FOREVER

my lady

C. Wilson

Forever My Lady
Copyright© 2024
C. WILSON

Follow C. Wilson on social media

Instagram: @authorcwilson

Facebook: Author C. Wilson

Join my reading group on Facebook:

Cecret Discussionz

Follow my reading group on Instagram:

@CecretDiscussionz

🌾 🌾 🌾 🌾 🌾 🌾

Tell me what you think of this story in a

customer review.

Thank you,

-xoxo-

C. Wilson

LETTER TO MY READERS

I already know what you were thinking: where is my favorite author? Well, here I am. I took this time out not only to rebrand myself but to reevaluate my writing style and techniques. The hiatus was needed for me to become better. With that being said… you already know what I am about to say. So go ahead and get your snack, drink, smoke, whatever your preference is. Make sure the kids or your boo is taken care of. Get in that self-love mood, light that candle, and grab that blanket. These new characters have become a breath of fresh air for me. Hopefully, you fall in love with Autumn and Patience how I have…

-xoxo-

C. Wilson

Forever *my lady* Playlist

Scared of Lonely, Beyoncé

Crying Out For Me, Mario

Permission, Ro James

Naked, Ella Mai

One Of Them Days, *Kiana Ledé*

Promises, *Photos*

Fall Slowly, *Joyner Lucas ft. Ashanti*

Bare Wit Me, *Teyana Taylor*

Whatever U Need, *Grimm Lynn*

Take Care Of You, *Charlotte Day Wilson ft. Syd*

Wake Up Love, *Teyana Taylor ft. Iman*

Higher, *Tems*

Love Listens, *Ahji*

Hold On, We're Going Home, *Drake ft. Majid Jordan*

Breathe Me, *Sia*

Take Care, *Drake ft. Rihanna*

Call On Me, *Janet Jackson ft. Nelly*

You Got It, *Vedo*

Spread Thin, *Mariah the Scientist*

H20, *Tink*

Heartbreak Anniversary, *Giveon*

Love Story/Interlude, *Rod Wave*

Comfortable, *H.E.R*

Trust, *Brent Faiyaz*

Heart Attack, *Trey Songz*

Spotify Playlist

Apple Music Playlist

SYNOPSIS

Autumn, a survivor of an abusive relationship, finds solace in the arms of Patience, a kind-hearted single father. With her ex refusing to let go, their love becomes a dangerous game. Can Patience protect Autumn and his child from the clutches of her obsessive ex, or will their love be doomed from the start?

Chapter 1

Autumn McKinley

The feeling of a clean house and clean sheets always did it for me. To top it off, lighting that candle once the task of cleaning down every nook and cranny of your house is complete just puts the cherry on top. I stared at the broken pieces of glass in the nearby dustpan as the night before replayed in my head…

"Lamar, stop, you're hurting me."

I shrieked when my back slammed into the Swiss coffee-colored walls behind me. The gold accented mirror I had handpicked from Hobby Lobby had fallen off the wall and shattered on impact when it collided with the Jacobean-stained hardwood flooring.

"Why do you always try and leave me?"

He questioned, and when I looked deep into his ruinous, evil eyes, I saw that he genuinely wanted an answer.

Lamar was my college sweetheart, and things between us were not always as bad as they were now. At the beginning of our love story, Lamar was sweet, gentle, and attentive to all my needs. Granted, he didn't have to meet many needs because, at twenty years old, I was just now becoming a woman, so I didn't have a lengthy list of them. With the age of thirty-three just around the corner, my wants for this relationship had changed, and he couldn't seem to understand that outgrowing people was a thing.

When I turned thirty, it was like I had an epiphany. All of the things I once tolerated I no longer felt the need to have in my presence. I heavily expressed that I felt us growing apart, and that is when the physical abuse came into play. Mentally, he couldn't control me, so I figured that getting me to submit by physical abuse was his only way. Growing up with someone from a young adult had taught me that over the years, I had allowed so much crap simply because of the bond that we once shared. I had to learn the hard way that Lamar was never a blessing. He was nothing more than a polished lesson. He looked good as hell to the eye, but his soul wasn't any good.

"Answer my question, Autumn," he demanded.

His deep baritone shook the walls around us as he tried to pull answers from me. If his screaming wouldn't get the answer he needed, his tight grip around my arms sure would. I quickly thought about the bruised rings that would quickly show if I didn't answer his question with speed.

"This is not love, and you know it. Just let me go. Just leave," I huffed, trying to catch my breath from our little scuffle. We had been going at it all morning, and I was tired.

The apartment we had occupied in Tucker for the past seven years was in my name. He was originally from Washington, D.C., while I was from New York. Once we had graduated, collectively, we had come up with the idea to move from the busy city to the south. Lamar had family in the Peach State, while all I had was him. I'm sure he could crash at his brother's house until he devised a game plan for his life.

Although he had problems with his family, he had one, and that was more than I could say for myself. His mother had died a couple of years ago, so his younger brother was the closest thing he had since his daddy had run for the hills the moment that his younger brother was born.

Outside of that, he had me, but I was done with being tied to him. I was standing firm on ending things with him. The three broken ribs from earlier this year immensely helped with that decision. When each argument turned into a fight, I had him pack up some of his things and remove them from my premises. I was weak in the knees and allowed him to come back numerous times after each fight, but I was done with that now.

What was left of his things could fit inside one of my chest drawers; today, he was leaving with that. What had started this fight was the simple fact that I had packed the rest of his things. Based on history, I had dragged out this relationship longer than needed. I was sick and tired of living for the memories of how we used to be when so much had changed over the years.

"I already called your coworkers. Just go," I muttered.

I had to let him know that I had called into the law. Those boys in blue were supposed to serve and protect the community, but they protected him more than anything else because they were his colleagues. That's another reason why I stayed and endured so much as long as I did. Lamar was part of Dekalb's County finest.

He landed the job when we first moved to Georgia. I remember filing a report on him a year prior that went nowhere. Of course, after filing the complaint, I took his sorry ass back, and that's when he explained everything to me. Later, I learned that his Captain had informed him to 'stay out of trouble' because he couldn't keep sweeping his personal life under the corrupt rug on which he had built his career.

Since that incident, Lamar walked cautiously each time I rushed to a phone during one of our fights. Feeling defeated, he finally released his tight grip on my arms.

"So, you really don't love me anymore?" he asked in his deep baritone.
The question wasn't hard to answer because, over the years, the love started to fade as the bruises, broken bones, and scars started to appear.

Lamar was a handsome man. Standing at 6'4, he hovered over my 5'6 stature. His butterscotch skin tone looked soft to the touch. His chiseled jawline made him appear meaner than he was. I knew the real, though. Not only was he mean, he was a sadistic asshole. He was a natural, pretty boy, and he held all the features of one, but his actions were the opposite.

Although he had a pretty exterior, his rough edge attracted me from day one. A coat of gloss covered his eyes as he waited for my response. I learned that those crocodile tears didn't mean anything. So many times, he tried to reel me in with that ploy to get me to feel bad for him. To get me to take him back. To get me to stay. And for years, it had worked. I looked deep into his dark brown eyes because I wanted him to get what I was saying loud and clear. I wanted him to understand that I was done. For real, this time.

"I stopped loving you the moment you were responsible for killing our baby."

I still remember the exact moment when I realized that the man standing in front of me was no longer my future. Earlier this year, when he had fractured three of my ribs, I discovered during my hospital visit that on top of the broken bones and bruises, I was also going through a miscarriage. What I thought was a heavy period was indeed me losing a life. I was ten weeks pregnant and didn't even know it. Fighting for my life daily was one hell of a distraction, I guess.

As quickly as the gloss covered what would appear to be sorrow-filled eyes, rage replaced it.

Lamar placed his hand around my throat and began to squeeze.

KNOCK KNOCK KNOCK

"Police open up."

Saved, I thought as he released the grip he had around my neck and then pushed me toward the ground. I struggled to catch my breath as he picked up the last bag of things he had in my place and then walked toward the front door...

Quickly, I picked up the dustpan and dumped the shards of glass into the nearby garbage can. Metaphorically I was tossing out my past, and it felt damn good. I looked around at the space around me. Although it was elegantly decorated, the emptiness that I felt in the pit of my stomach was something that I could not shake.

I was accustomed to having a body lay beside me every night. I was used to picking up balled-up socks off the floor and putting the toilet seat down before I used the bathroom. Living with a man had become second nature to me.

That's another reason I had stayed in an unhealthy relationship for so long. I was petrified of being lonely. I really wanted to know why I was like this. The feeling of being alone scared me to death, but it was a feeling I was going to have to embrace because I wanted to be better for myself. I needed to be better for myself.

I opened one of the windows to let some of the summer's fresh air in. I yawned because I was exhausted from cleaning the entire house. I put anything that would remind me of Lamar by the front door. In a sense, while cleaning the house, I was also cleaning out my soul.

At the end of my exasperated sigh, I felt a pain in my jawline that I knew only came from our previous fight. In my mind, I had won the battle, but something told me that the war was only beginning. Lamar was not the kind of man who was easy at letting things go, so I'm sure I had a long road ahead.

I remember that in college, I tried breaking up with him. He had beaten the poor boy up that I tried to move on with. Literally, he had pulled the boy out of his car and then had beaten him so severely that he had to get hospitalized. From then on, I should have run away and never looked back, but no, I had this nagging attachment to him. Over the years, I had tried so hard to be everything he wanted that I had forgotten who I was.

It was time for me to get back to Autumn. I need to reintroduce myself back to the confident, sexy woman that didn't take any shit. Getting over him and sticking to my guns would be easier said than done. It was an uphill climb that I was prepared for, though. I walked to my master bathroom and then ran myself some bath water.

I needed to soak my aching bones, and a day nap was calling me badly. I was glad that I had taken the day off. I tried my hardest not to call in, but when we had a big fight like this, whatever job I was working never saw me the next day because I needed a good twenty-four hours to get together. I just knew that tomorrow was going to whoop me.

☙ ☙ ☙ ☙ ☙ ☙

Staring at the clock was doing nothing but letting my shift at work go by even slower. I had prepared the attorney that I worked for case files, and they were sitting at his desk, waiting for him to go over them. Working at Johnson and Jacobs could go by slowly at times, but it was peaceful because it was away from home. Although I had done all my work for the day, I quickly busied myself when my boss walked through the doors.

"Mr. Jacobs, your case files are on your desk," I said quickly as he breezed past.

He gave me a head nod before going into his office and closing the door. He wasn't a man of many words, so over the past two years of my job, he opted for head nods, and we shared the bare minimum. Small talk came and went, but when I think of it, I didn't know much about my employer. He was a very handsome man, but I'm sure that his attitude wasn't worth a damn.

That man walked around with deep brown almond-shaped eyes. Those pupils paired well with his deep, dark skin complexion. Men that looked that good usually had the unfortunate trait of being stuck up. Not to mention that his bushy caterpillar brows always looked arched in anger.

He was intimidating to talk to, so I opted for quick statements since I had gotten hired. He seemed all about his business; I had to respect that. Coming from working inside a catty work environment like the post office to this one, I understood the importance of discreetness. This job definitely changed the scenery and vibes. Granted, I had only worked at the post office during the holiday season, but it was enough to let me know that kind of work environment wasn't for me.

After getting laid off from that job, I had odd ones and did Instacart and Doordash until I saw an opening for my current position. It was easy money because I was naturally organized and professional. I think it was the Capricorn energy in me. One thing I had always been goal-driven. I quickly learned that a degree obtained in college didn't mean a real thing in the real world unless you had the work experience to go with it.

Majoring in business management didn't mean anything because I had taken a break after college to help Lamar get through his police academy. I was blessed to have landed a job like the one I had. I caught the company when they were up and coming, and I am glad I had. Although an intimate office, Jackson and Jacobs was one of Atlanta's most prestigious practices. The workload wasn't much, but I liked it. With a job like this, the day went by quickly or slowly.

For the remainder of the day, I had busied myself with notes that Mr. Jackson had left behind for me. He was actually the man responsible for hiring me. I was the only secretary when I started, with Mr. Jackson and Mr. Jacobs being the only divorce attorneys. A year after I started, they hired two other lawyers and one secretary to work alongside me. Amani had become more than a coworker; she had also become a good friend.

"We only got an hour left," she said with relief.

I had picked my head up from my arm fort and saw a cup of coffee waiting for me on the edge of the French imported desk. Being one of the employees present during the start-up, I had little say in the office. The design of the place was one of them. By the time Amani had gotten hired, everything was where it needed to be. She must have known that today was getting the best of me. The cup of brew was needed.

"Thank you," I said with a kind smile.

She sat in the seat behind her desk and then rolled over in my direction.

"So did you kick his trifling ass out?" she whispered.

She knew everything when it came to Lamar and me. I shook my head up and down and then took a small sip from the coffee she had gotten me. I was careful not to burn my upper lip with the steam from the heat.

"I'm proud of you, girly. That's one step closer in the right direction. You deserve a love that doesn't hurt. When I say that, I mean physically and emotionally."

A small smile appeared across my face because Amani had one of those healing spirits. I don't know if she knew this, but she was one of the main reasons I had enough courage to be done with Lamar. She was a *take-no-shit* woman, and I loved that about her. I could tell that her grandmother was the kind that used to throw hot grits on a man for doing her wrong.

She walked in the spirit of strong ancestors. I, on the other hand, aspired to be that. My mother used to get her ass handed to her by every stepfather that I had, and my grandmother was no better. The abuse between her and my granddad is what started the cycle that the McKinley women couldn't seem to break from. Being the only child, I was going to break that, though. Unlike my grandmother and mother, I wasn't going to allow someone's nappy-headed son to put me on a t-shirt.

You think that with me both losing my grandmother and then mother to domestic violence, I would have strayed far away from it. I guess a piece of me didn't mind the suffocating space in between playing with my life and not.

"I know. Thank you for always reminding me," I thanked.

I never had planned on getting this close to a coworker, but Amani had this aura about her that pulled you in and kept you there.

A few months ago, she noticed a ring around my neck after one of our fights from Lamar choking me. Never did her eyes show judgment or disdain. She just discreetly ushered me to the bathroom and offered some of her concealer and foundation. Since we had the same mocha complexion, her makeup matched my skin.

We had spent ten minutes in the small office restroom while I basically had an emotional breakdown. Amani did not interrupt my choked-up, teary breakdown, nor did she make me feel lesser than her. We walked in as just two coworkers and walked out with a bond that couldn't be broken. She had become the younger sister I never had and never knew I needed.

My being six years her senior didn't affect our bond. For her to only be twenty-six years old, she was well beyond her years. Her small stature was nothing compared to her bigger-than-life personality. She was spicy and very opinionated. Again, her aura is truly something.

"Well, now that you're done with that, you can—"

She cut her own words short and then scooted back to her desk when Mr. Jacobs quickly walked out of his office and headed toward the front door. Another thing that I appreciated was that she understood and respected the art of discreteness. With a relaxed work environment most of the day, we spent it gossiping but never around the attorneys.

"Are you done for the day?" I mustered up to ask Mr. Jacobs as he rushed past. He seemed to always be on the go, which made it hard to speak to him. Again, sometimes, he was so intimidating to talk to.

"Yes, goodnight, ladies."

In unison, we both said goodnight to him.

"Ms. McKinley, your boss is fineeeee," Amani sang out once Mr. Jacobs was out of the office.

Most days, he was one of the first attornies to come in and the last to leave. Amani was right; he looked good. To be honest, the men that we worked for were very handsome. Both men were easy to look at. Mr. Jacobs had this chocolate skin tone, while Mr. Jackson possessed a caramel-colored complexion.

Being self-made, successful, black, and sexy, I knew both had to be taken. Single men with that kind of criteria were rare in Atlanta. Women out here scouted those kinds of men in college, dug their claws into them, and never let go. I didn't blame them either. In college, you were supposed to lock in with who had enough potential to be the love of your life. Or at least lock in with a candidate with enough credentials to benefit your life.

Other women had the right idea, while I, on the other hand, made the decision to lock in with a bum. I appreciated being around both Mr. Jacobs and Mr. Jackson because it raised my bar of aspirations.

"He's your boss too," I giggled, just thinking of how hard Mr. Jacobs had to have been goal-driven to accomplish as much as he had so far.

"Yeah, but he doesn't let me tend to his files. He leaves that task for you and you only."

Although very sweet, Amani was very forgetful, and Mr. Jacobs didn't play when it came to his work.

"You need to let his fine ass tend to that womanly area between your legs. Let a real man fondle that kitty kat," she joked.

Her motto was to get over one; you had to get under another, and she never let a chance go by without reminding me of that. I shook my head and smirked, trying my hardest not to let my face blush. You could tell that God took his time when he made Mr. Jacobs.

From his chiseled features down to his build, he was well thought of before being constructed in God's lab. I bet the man above sat with a pen and pad for months, maybe years, before working on him. Perfection is what he looked like to me, and Amani had to think the same way with the way that she openly lusted over him.

That man was so fine. I bet his halo would have diamonds and gems when he died and went to heaven. I always caught a whiff of his designer scent. Off looks alone, he was deserving of the finer things. He definitely had the job, and judging by the midnight blue Mercedes that he drove, I knew he preferred the finer things in life.

Men of his caliber had their life together and knew exactly what they wanted. Men of his caliber didn't necessarily need a woman for anything. I had a thing for running away from men that didn't need someone. A woman who lived check to check with an abusive ex was probably the furthest thing on men with standards radar.

"I bet he has a girlfriend," I said as if I had a chance with a man of his making.

I had this thing for doubting myself. I knew I was a pretty girl, but I had that sad-ass build a nigga up mentality, so whenever I did come across a man with some kind of substance, I pushed them away. When I met Lamar in college, he was broke like me and had nothing going on with himself.

I was the one who convinced him to go into the criminal justice field. While we dated on and off in college, other men were trying to pursue me, but I had this thing for Lamar. Since the one time I tried to date someone worked out so horribly for me, I had never tried again.

I put my head down with pouty lips as I thought about one of my biggest mistakes. He, by far, was one of them.

"I bet the rest of these Atlanta women don't give a rat's ass about that. The women-to-men ratio here is horrible. Taking the incarcerated, undercover brothers and abusers off the table just made the numbers worse."

Amani did have a point. The women down here in Atlanta were vultures. Being from up north, I didn't have this problem.

Well, being in a relationship for so long had spoiled me in a sense because although I was getting my ass beat for the latter of the union, I was off the market. I didn't have to worry about being lied to or, worse, having my man be secretly gay or bisexual. Although Lamar had his ways of abuse, one thing that he wasn't was a liar. A man of mine living a double life was a fear of mine.

I personally didn't have a problem with gay men; I just wished that more of them in this congested city would live in their truth. Our little conversation had let the time pass, and before I knew it. It was time to go.

"Are you heading to the gym tonight?" Amani asked, changing the subject.

I had found solace in the gym because it was yet another place away from my toxic living situation.

Focusing on my body had become the norm because it gave me a mental escape that I desperately needed.

"Yup, my bag is already packed and in the car."

"That's right, mama, get that body right for your next man."

Amani again tossed in my face that laying up with the next man was the only way to get over Lamar. The last thing on my mind was a man, and considering how my last relationship went, I had a valid reason to think that way. We hugged briefly before I locked up the office. Mr. Jackson was on vacation, and I had to do this again in another fifteen hours.

The drive to the gym was quick since the distance between the two was only ten minutes. This was one of the reasons that I enjoyed the city. It reminded me so much of home since everything was so close together. When they moved to Georgia, many people moved to the outskirts and said Atlanta when someone asked because that's what most people knew.

I grabbed my gym bag from the back seat and scanned in before heading to the locker room to change. After getting into my gym clothes, I was pumped and ready to get a good workout. My specialty was cardio since I was trying to reach my goal of one hundred and sixty-five pounds. I was thirteen pounds away from my goal, so the Stairmaster had become my best friend. Whenever I came straight from work, all the machines were taken.

One guy was going to work on the machine. He had this sweater on with the hood tied tightly around his head. He was running up the damn stairs at full speed. He had to prepare his body to be a firefighter, or the Avengers needed another member, and he was training for that.

Either way, he was openly pushing his body to certain limits that I ran away from. Knowing no one would give up a machine anytime soon, I opted for the treadmill, elliptical, and bike. I was going to get a good workout in because, more than anything, it cleared my head so desperately that I wanted a clear mind.

Chapter 2

Patience Jacobs

"Push yourself. Nobody is going to want it if you don't want it."

"But I'm tired."

"Tired of what Parker?"

I scolded my daughter because her coach told me she had been falling behind in practice. I was dishing out money for a private coach and AAU fees all because my daughter wanted to be a WNBA player. She was damn good at the sport. She took after me for sure. She was a point guard with some handle, and at her age, most girls didn't learn the art of controlling the ball, let alone know the fundamentals of the sport.

Not only could she have and take control of the ball, but she could also dribble. A little piece of me was happy when she liked the sport. Secretly, I could live vicariously through her. There were so many of my life goals that I had tweaked and altered once she had come into my life.

I had plans to play basketball overseas, but my dream took a backseat when she was born ten years ago. Instead of leaving college to fulfill my dream, I changed my major from sports medicine to law. I was thankful that my mom was my personal village because she stepped in when raising Parker. After years of practicing, I opened my firm alongside Matthew, one of my best friends from high school.

I set the bar damn high when it came to education. One thing I loved about my child is that just as enthusiastic as she was about her sport, she was the same regarding her schoolwork. She had been on the honor roll since starting school in Pre-K. I prided myself when it came to the part that I played in my daughter's life, and she didn't even know that as a man, I was better in every way because she was in mine.

Being a single parent was unexpected, to say the least. When Parker's mother, Ayesha, was pregnant with her, I thought that would be my happily ever after. Badly, I wanted to finish things with the person with whom I had started everything. I was sure that Parker's mother would be my wife one day. Boy, was I wrong. The woman turned out to be batshit crazy. When Parker was about four months old, I saw that her mother not only didn't have our daughter's best interest at heart, but she had grown a resentment for the baby once my attention shifted from her to Parker.

An adult being jealous of a baby was insane to me. Picking up on that early, I ended things with her and filed for full custody of Parker. Because my life was more together than hers after we split, I was granted custody. I thought that her sudden disinterest had a lot to do with postpartum stress. For a while, I still tried to make things work because the last thing that I wanted was to be one of those insensitive asshole ass dudes after their girl had a baby.

In time, I started to see that she had no intention of being a parent. It must have been a weight lifted off her shoulders once she was legally no longer responsible for Parker because the ink on the custody papers hadn't even dried yet before she totally abandoned her own child. She had blocked my number and damn near fell off the face of this earth. We haven't heard from her for nine years, and I preferred it that way. I don't need nor want any fake love around my baby. I protected and somewhat sheltered Parker because, unlike other children her age, she didn't have that mother in her life.

"Tired of what, Parker," I repeated myself when I saw tears dripping down the cheeks of the mini version of me.

She had my high cheekbones and even my shaped eyes. She got her caramel complexion from my mother. I looked fixedly at my daughter and saw that although she had resembled me and my mother for all of her life, I couldn't deny that she was starting to grow into her mother when it came to her looks.

"Of running," she whimpered out.

I turned off the treadmill and leaned against the gym's wall in our housing complex. I had just done eighty damn flights in ten minutes on the Stairmaster at Planet Fitness. The last thing I wanted to hear was how she was tired of running in our community gym.

The spot I had resided in for the past year was a hidden gem, especially with all the upgrades they had made around the property. We had the luxury of enjoying the gym, pool, tennis, and basketball court.

"Your coach said you were walking all practice, so I know you're not tired of running. You haven't even stepped foot on the treadmill yet."

I made sure not to raise my tone but to speak sternly to her. The way I parented was different than how I was raised because my mother would have slapped me upside the back of the head and then told me to still run. Parker was unique, though. Although she had her rough ways and could hang with the toughest of boys, I still handled her with care because she was still a girl at the end of the day. My little girl.

On top of that, naturally, my baby girl was sensitive. Not having her mother around definitely opened a door of emotions that I was still trying to get a handle on. My mother had suggested therapy for her to work through those emotions, but I felt as if I had things under control, at least for right now.

"You need to tell me if basketball isn't your thing anymore. I can save my money, and your coaches and grandmother can save their time," I said calmly.

I wished she wasn't trying to give up on the sport. She had so much potential to go to waste if she made that decision. But, unlike most parents, I was giving her the choice to decide what she wanted to do. One thing that I wasn't going to do was guilt trip my child into doing anything that she didn't want to do.

"No, I want to play," she said with confidence.

"Then act like it," I said with a slight smirk because she had drive like me too.

She used the back of her hands to wipe away those crocodile tears, and then she hopped on the treadmill and did her thing. I stood back and recorded her hard work and dedication, which I made a mental note to post on her Instagram account later. Parker was a dog when it came to basketball, and she honestly loved the sport.

After a quick thirty-minute workout, I had to get her in the house and get her ready for school the next day. Being a single parent isn't for the weak, so our schedule was gridlocked with minimum deviations. We walked from the gym to our home while she talked with my mother on the phone.

"I did good today on my workout, Grandma."

"Did you? Daddy didn't push you too hard, did he? Cause I'll have to put my foot up his ass."

Parker's almond-shaped eyes rolled over in my direction. She batted those long lashes she got from me before covering her mouth as if that would silence her response.

"He was a little rough, but not so much."

"Well, that's good, Pumpkin. I miss you guys, and I'll be home by the time you get out of school tomorrow."

"Miss you too! Daddy, say bye to grandma," Parker turned her phone in my direction, and I saw her on a Facebook video call with my mother.

"Bye, Ma."

My mother blew kisses into the camera before ending the line. It killed me how soft and delicate my mother was with Parker. When me and my brother were growing up, she was the cornrow version of Queen Latifa, but now that she was a grandmother, her ass dropped the gutter Cleo from Set It Off act and brought out the silk-pressed version of Dana Owens.

Not to mention that out of nowhere, she became the kind of parent with McDonald's money. I was grateful that she stepped up when it came to Parker. She tried her best to fill whatever void could possibly be left behind by Parker's mother not being present. I appreciated the fuck out of her for it because she had a lot going on in her own personal life, and she never missed a beat when it came to my daughter.

After beating cancer the year prior, my mother had been traveling the world. I don't blame her either. After receiving the devastating news, it literally shook our entire world up. I was raised by my mother and grandmother because, at a young age, my father was murdered in a hit-and-run accident. I wasn't close to my dad before his passing, so all I had was my mother and grandmother. Just the thought of losing one of them shook me to my core.

When the news of my mom's cancer came, we made the executive decision as a family to collide in households. My younger brother was off doing his own thing, so I stepped up and handled everything regarding my mother. Making the decision to live together took a lot of thought, but it couldn't have come at a better time.

Not only did it save us money, but I could keep a watchful eye on my mother, which I felt was much needed. I was going through a breakup then, so the decision made sense. On some *Wizard of Oz* shit, there was no place like home. To me, home was wherever my mom was.

"Parker, get in the shower before you walk in that kitchen," I told her as soon as we walked in the door.

The beautiful thing about raising an athlete was the amount of food that they ate. When I say this, I say it with every sarcastic bone in my body. This little girl put away food like a grown man.

"Okay, Daddy, can we have buffalo chicken bites for dinner?"

"Yeah, that's cool."

I got into the kitchen, washed my hands, and tossed a few in the air fryer. Like Parker, I was excited for my mother's return because I wasn't much of a cook. She was the cook in the household, and when she went on her vacations, Parker and I opted for quick meals.

When I heard Parker turn the water off, I tossed her chicken bites into a bowl. I needed a shower myself. The weightlifting I did after work had the sweat that clung to my frame make my skin crawl. I took the BBQ sauce from the pantry and tossed it onto the granite countertop. My kid had weird eating habits, so I knew she would ask for the sauce once she got her bowl.

"Your food is on the counter," I called out just before going to my bedroom and closing the door behind me.

A frustrated sigh escaped my lips once the door closed. I never understood what it meant when mothers said that they needed some me time until I became a single parent myself. Being the oldest sibling, I remember seeing my moms crack with the pressure of raising my brother and me alone, but one thing she never did was break.

With my father dead and my little brother's father doing life in prison, all she had was her mother, my grandmother. I had one child, and she was responsible for two in a similar situation. That alone showed me that I could do it. I felt like I had been running since before the sun came up, and here it was, the sun setting, and I was just now ending my day.

I looked at my Xbox and second-guessed, hopping on 2K with the boys before my shower. A couple of the guys from back home and I played the game often, and I knew that around this time, they would be looking for me to be on, but I was truly exhausted. I needed to play catch up on some rest.

My room was off by itself, so it didn't matter what Parker was doing before bed. It didn't disturb me, and I could sleep peacefully. I had this side of the house all to myself. Before moving in, my mother and I had agreed that I would take the master bedroom because it had the bathroom attached to it. She said she and Parker could share a bathroom since they were both females.

For the most part, this side of the house belonged to me. I had direct access to the front door, so if the possibility of company ever came, I would have some form of privacy. I didn't have to worry about that because dating was the last thing on my mind. I was almost a year out of a divorce, and my focus now was on me and my child. Things between my ex-wife, Tonya, and I had ended when I realized she was jealous of my relationship with my mother and daughter. It was the weirdest thing ever to me.

Every single woman that I had come across had either had a problem with me being a single parent or had a problem with how much my mother helped me with raising Parker. I had been told that I was less of a man because of the amount of assistance that my mother rendered. The whole shit was bananas, if you ask me. To me, that was equivalent to having a problem with my child and my mother, and any woman who thought that she was going to toe with either one of them was a goner.

Tonya had slipped through the cracks for so long because she put on this façade at the beginning of our relationship. She had a girl and a child of her own, and in the beginning, things between her daughter and Parker were amazing. That was until it wasn't. After getting married, Tonya tried to make it seem like I spoiled my daughter more than hers, but that wasn't the case. My child was in a sport that required more than just toys. Uniforms, accessories, and the whole nine had to be purchased.

I even suggested that she put her daughter in a sport or activity so that things could seem even, but all my suggestions went on deaf ears. Like the others, my mother's assistance in raising my daughter was also a problem. That could be because, toward the end of our marriage, I started to see that Tonya had a control problem. I ended things when all the nagging and bickering became too much for me.

One thing I was big on was my peace, and it had taken me a long time to get this way, so believe me when I say that anything and anyone will get the boot when that is in jeopardy. With ease, I had tossed a four-year relationship, one in which I was married entirely down the drain without care. To say that we could only celebrate one wedding anniversary was honestly pathetic.

It helped that I was a divorce attorney, and one of my best friends was one. So, I had Matthew head our divorce, and luckily, I had a prenup in place before our marriage. My mother had taught me to always protect my assets. She had retired from being an accountant for this global finance company, so she knew a little about how to keep a penny or two.

This is why I knew my mother wouldn't when every woman failed me when managing finances. I was the kind of guy comfortable with making the money and handing it over to my partner to handle business. Although I was in the 21st century when it came to dating, I still had domestic old-fashioned ways for me. I was a natural-born provider, and I just preferred to be with a woman who was at least responsible enough to make sure that bills were paid with the money that I had provided.

Tonya couldn't manage shit, and to be irresponsible with a control problem was a dangerous combination. I was glad that I had no ties with her when the divorce was final. When Avant said, '*every time I see you, I get a bad vibe,*' I felt that in my soul. You can catch me humming along every time it comes on. That's how badly the entire song resonates with my whole being.

After we had gone our separate ways, I had heard through the grapevine that she had moved back up north, and I was relieved for that. When I say that I heard through the grapevine, I mean that my brother's third baby mama was yapping on the phone with my mother and relaying a message that wasn't needed. She took every chance that she could to talk shit about her sister.

I shook off the ill thoughts of Tonya and her family drama that I was happy to be rid of and then walked to my bathroom to turn on the shower.

Knock Knock

Damn, I thought to myself just as I was checking the temperature of my water.

"Daddy? Can I use your headphones?"

I let Parker's question linger for a bit before I pulled my room door open. She was raised to wait at a door until it was opened or she was granted permission to enter.

So, I didn't have the problem of her busting in my room at her own will. I had purchased more than enough headphones for her, so why she needed mine was beyond me, but I was in no mood to play the investigation game with her.

"Here, make sure you put them on the charger when you are finished."

I handed her my gym headphones and then quickly closed the door back. That's another thing I had to quickly learn about this single-parent thing. There was no such thing as a moment to yourself when you had a little one in the house. Although Parker was more independent than other children her age, she was still a child, so she was still very needy.

After pulling my gym clothes off my frame, I stood in the mirror to check my progress with my body goals. My abs were coming back, and I had worked damn hard for them. I had lost myself a bit after that divorce, so it felt good to see that my hard work was paying off. Although ultimately, the decision was mine to end the marriage, I still went through the motions because initially, I had gotten married to stay that way, but hey, shit happens.

When I got in the shower, I put my entire head under the stainless steel dual shower head. I let the steamy beads ease some of the tension out of my muscles. The next day was going to be a long one, and I needed to be well-rested since I had to sit in court damn near all day. When I finished washing, I tossed on some pajamas, laid in my bed, and then posted Parker's content until bedtime. Since our schedule was so tight, I knew Parker had fallen asleep before me when I heard her television turn off an hour before mine.

※ ※ ※ ※ ※

"Where's Autumn?" When I came out of my office for the third time, I asked Amani when I noticed she was nowhere in sight.

"I'm not sure I called twice," a panic in Amani's tone made me raise my eyebrow in suspicion.

It was unlike her to be late. She had called out the day before yesterday, and even that was uncommon. Earlier this year, she took some vacation days, which I immediately approved since she didn't miss work. Autumn was definitely heaven-sent. During the last two years of her work for me, she kept all my files nice and organized. She always provided me with the coffee I needed but never asked for, and tracked all my meetings and court dates.

When it came to answering the phone and leaving messages, she left them so detailed that when I called clients back, I knew exactly what it was about. I checked the time on my Movado watch and noticed I had to be in court in about an hour. I would give her another ten minutes before there would be a problem with me and her about her tardiness.

Although her actions this morning were uncommon, I was a man all about my business, and being late without notice was unacceptable. I learned that being slack on rules could cause chaos, and I'll be damned if everything I had worked so hard for went to the shitter.

Something about how Amani looked at me always made me slightly uncomfortable, so I waited in my office while letting the ten minutes pass. Matthew was responsible for hiring, and I wouldn't have hired Amani personally. Although she was a sweet girl, she was a natural born fuck up.

At the time of our opening, we had shit all over the place, so even after hiring Autumn, we were still in dire need of someone else. Matthew tried hiring one of his cousins to help her, but I immediately fired her when I caught her stealing office supplies. There was no way that Autumn could do it all, so Matthew had the bright idea of hiring another secretary. I was cool with it as long as it wasn't one of his family members.

Amani misplaced notes and took down wrong messages when she took calls. Matt kept her around because she was nice to look at. Her little frame owned a pair of double D's and wide hips that she must have had handed down from her mother or grandmother. She didn't have much totting behind her, but the natural frame she walked around with in a world of BBL Barbies was refreshing. She had this country drawl that I could tell she worked hard to tame because we were in a professional setting.

As soon as I realized she couldn't cut it when it came to being a secretary, I was glad I already had Autumn. So, I let Matthew deal with Amani. A couple of times, the two of them messing around crossed my mind, but I decided not to ask about it because what my best friend wanted me to know, he would share in due time. They had this weird work relationship, and I knew Matthew had been a flirt since high school, but I figured asking his college sweetheart to marry him would have calmed him down.

I shook his business from my thoughts because it wasn't for me to worry about what he had going on. I was squeezing my stress ball and slowly spinning back and forth in the chair behind my desk as I waited for Autumn's arrival. I heard her rushing in when the clock went down to two minutes left.

"Girl, I've been calling you," I overheard Amani say.

There was a fear in her voice that I personally felt was overly dramatic. Naturally, she was theatrical, though. For her to be so small, she had this bigger-than-life personality.

"I'm okay. I just… I had a flat tire this morning. It was a lot going on. Did Mr. Jacobs leave for court alr—"

I ended her speaking by talking loud enough for her to hear me.

"Autumn, a word, in my office."

I swear you could hear a needle drop in the parking lot outside with how quiet both ladies had gotten.

I picked my head out of my phone when I saw through my peripheral vision that Autumn was standing in the doorway of my office. She slowly closed my office door behind her to give us privacy so I could scold her. Autumn looked frazzled, but I still took in her beauty. Since she had started, I caught myself stealing little glances at her just to admire her aura. Tonya and I were already on the outs when Autumn had started, so steeling glances had become my guilty pleasure. Her brown skin always looked like shea butter was her best friend, and she always held a bit of gloss on her juicy lips.

She had done the makeup thing occasionally, but for the most part, she opted for the natural look, and I secretly loved that. Being that I was a stickler for keeping the work environment how it should be, I never looked at her for longer than a minute. As the months passed, I caught myself looking at her for more extended periods. *She's so fucking pretty,* I thought as I watched her openly wearing her nerves in front of me. She rubbed both hands down her burgundy pencil skirt to iron it out.

"Yes, Mr. Jacobs," there was an anxious sound to her.

I nodded toward the stack of case files on the edge of my desk.

"Is that everything that I need for court today?"

I already checked over them three times, but I just wanted to ask briefly to give myself more time to look at her.

"It is. The files should be in the order of your cases today."

"Okay."

"Okay?" she questioned as if I would have had something else to add.

Under normal circumstances, I would have had a lot to say, but like I said, her absence the other day and tardiness from this morning were unlike her. My crushing on her for the past two years allowed me to let her slide. I noticed her rubbing her arms. I'm sure she was trying to rid her body of goosebumps due to the cool temperature of the office. It didn't matter if it was winter or summer outside the office; it always held this frigid temperature.

Matthew was scared to have it warm in the office after the Corona outbreak because he said keeping it cold kept the germs out. We actually had to push our grand opening back because of it. He had the office cold as hell, and I mean, a hospital cold. Usually, Autumn wore a sweater or cardigan, but on this day, she did not. She was rubbing her arms at a speed that held my attention. I spotted a ring around the top of her arm, instantly infuriating me.

It looked like a bruise. I was a natural-born protector, so I had to take a moment to remember that this was my employee and whatever she had going on was none of my business. Still, my battle with addressing the bruise was evident in how my thick eyebrows dipped, causing a scowl to plaster my face.

"Is is that all?" Her stuttering caused me to look from her arm to her face.

"Uhh yeah, that's it."

Evidently, I had made her uncomfortable and intended to address it. Although she was just my employee, she was a good girl with a heart of gold, so I was willing to extend that olive branch and offer some of my assistance if needed. *I can protect you. All you need to do is ask.* I somehow wished that she could read my thoughts. Women like her didn't deserve to be a doormat or punching bag to a nigga. No woman deserved that shit. Like I said, women raised me, so I valued and worshiped the ground they had walked on.

As black men, we were great because we came from black women. Any man putting their hands on them didn't understand that. Ten minutes in a room with whoever was responsible for placing the ring on Autumn's arm was all that I needed to show his ass that fundamental rule. That was a talk and a battle for another time because I didn't want to be late for court. I grabbed the case files and then headed out the door.

Chapter 3

Autumn

I watched as Mr. Jacobs hurried out to head to court. I snatched my cardigan off the back of my chair and quickly put it on. Catching a flat tire on the way in really made me out of place and threw me off my whole morning. I could tell by how he looked down at my arm that he was passing judgment on me.

I knew that I would bruise from when Lamar and I fought, and since the office would usually be chilly, it was rare that I was seen inside without a long sleeve of some sort. I rushed into the building so quickly I had forgotten to cover up. I had forgotten to hide the parts of me that I had been hiding from the world for the past two years.

"Were you able to have AAA at least come and put the spare on?" Amani asked once I took a seat at my desk.

"No, I left it on the side of the road and took an Uber. I didn't want to be too late and possibly lose this job. With Lamar and me being done, I need this money more than anything."

That is one thing I hated about returning to a one-income household. Everything was on me, and I didn't have anyone else to look to. There was no 50/50 at my disposal any longer. Waiting for AAA could quickly turn into an all-day task, especially with the traffic in Atlanta, and I couldn't have that. Amani stopped smiling at her phone for a second to offer me a response.

"Girl, call AAA and have them at least tow it somewhere. These fools will steal your car and sell the parts for money."

Instantly, I started to panic because although I had been in Atlanta for some years, there was still so much I didn't know about the city. I barely visited the actual city unless Lamar took us there. My little Jeep Renegade wasn't my preferred vehicle when I got it, but it was great on gas, and I worked my ass off to get it.

The last thing I needed was some teenagers tearing it apart for money. I opened the Geico app on my phone and scheduled my car to be picked up and towed to a nearby tire shop. They closed at seven, and I got off at five, so I had enough time to make it there. The day seemed to go by slowly, and I dreaded it.

"Do you think that he was mad at me this morning?" I randomly asked Amani.

"Huh?"

She seemed confused and had all right to be because I had blurted the statement out after a long silence. Something about how Mr. Jacobs looked at me when I entered his office earlier had me sitting on the edge of my seat. I didn't know if he had planned on disciplinary action for my tardiness.

"Mr. Jacobs..." I added to catch her up to speed.

"Autumn, you are human. People are late for work. I'm sure you are fine. It's not like you have a history of being a slacker."

I brushed off my worry about my job, and the phone started ringing just in time.

"Jackson and Jacobs law firm, this is Autumn speaking. How may I help you?" I answered in my chipper customer service tone. One thing about me was that I was a Brooklyn, New York girl to the bone. Still, when it came to my professionalism, my time at Howard University shined past the minor ghetto exterior I portrayed at times. There was a silence on the other end.

"Hello?" I repeated.

The eerie silence made my stomach feel funny. I quickly hung up the phone and then checked my cell phone. I haven't heard from Lamar, which was surprising.

"Who was that?" Amani asked as she still casually typed away on her phone.

"I don't know, probably a wrong number," I quickly responded as I attempted to brush off the feeling in my stomach.

Amani gave me this unsure look, but like me, she brushed the notion off. With Mr. Jackson returning from vacation tomorrow, there was still much that needed to be done before his return. For the rest of the day, I spent my time helping Amani sort through and complete all of the tasks that Mr. Jackson had left behind for her. He had been gone for the entire week, and she was just now getting around to the list of things he had left for her. A procrastinator was another thing that I would add to Amani's list of things that were wrong with her.

"This is so dumb. Having old case files in alphabetical order is out of control. I mean, they are old, right?" Amani complained.

"Being organized, period, as a lawyer is mandatory," I responded as I gathered a stack of old case files.

"Where did he go again?" Amani asked, I assumed referring to Mr. Jackson.

Although Mr. Jacobs wasn't much of a talker, his colleague was. I knew more about Mr. Jackson than I would have liked to. I shrugged my shoulders because half of what the man said to me I didn't retain.

"I forgot that his fine self is from up north. Isn't Mr. Jacobs from up north as well?"

For some odd reason, Amani had a lot of questions today. Not only did she have many questions, but she was basically talking to herself because my mind was preoccupied with how I would handle the bills I was now responsible for. I'm sure that my annoyance with her line of questioning had everything to do with my morning. I scrunched my face and tried to think hard about where Mr. Jacobs was from. I knew he had an accent from up north, but I wasn't sure where he came from.

"He probably is. He sounds like it," I finally responded after a brief silence.

My cellphone ringing caused me to drop one of the case files on Amani's desk and then head over to mine to stop the noise from my purse. Usually, I would keep my phone on silent, but my morning was all over the place. I couldn't even remember if I had put deodorant on because I was moving so quickly this morning.

"Hello?" I answered with suspicion due to the unsaved Georgia number.

"Ms. McKinley, we have your vehicle. Do you have plans on coming today for it?"

I had to give it to Geico, and they moved with urgency regarding the request I had put in about my vehicle. I honestly didn't know if I even had enough for the spare. The last thing I needed was to tack on storage fees.

"I'll be there around six. Is that okay?"

I still had to lock up and order an Uber to take me to the place. I could have asked Amani to drop me off, but I hated asking people for things. It didn't matter how close we were. There was a brief pause, and that is when I knew that this man was an asshole.

According to the Geico app, this shop didn't close until seven, so I had enough time to make it there. He gave a deep sigh before responding.

"Yeah, I guess that is fine."

He ended the line before I was given a chance to respond, and that pissed me off. I tossed my cell phone back into my bag before going back to help Amani with those case files.

🌿 🌿 🌿 🌿 🌿 🌿

Patience

I lightly tapped the pen in my hand on the oak desk in front of me. I was zoned out as the other divorce attorney gave his testimony on why his client should have full custody of the four-year-old child that was shared with my client. I preferred cases that could be settled outside the courtroom, but lately, I haven't been blessed with those. I was willing to take whatever would pay the bills, though.

One thing about me is that I didn't shy away from a case, no matter how difficult it was. I had this unbeatable streak and didn't plan to mess up my record any time soon. My client was being painted as an erratic, unstable woman after the split between her and her husband. The other attorney even had an officer come up and testify about his actions during the night of the split.

"Officer Hoover, recall your account of the night in question."

The other attorney had a personal vendetta against me because when it came to the inside of this courtroom, he had yet to beat me. When it came to my clients wanting financial stability and their children, I did my thing every time. I briefly listened to the officer state what he had responded to and how my client acted. His O'Shea Jackson Jr.-looking ass was laying it on thick with his testimony and making it seem like my client was a monster.

In all fairness, he probably was just recalling things as he remembered seeing them. Still, his side of the story made me wonder if the ending of my streak was closer than I thought. Beside me, my client hung her head low, and I hated the shit. I always vowed to myself that I would never let a woman let me crash out. I was raising a daughter alone, and the last thing that I needed was to be behind bars and taken away from her.

One of my worst fears was her being a child and not having me at her side. Outside of me, she had my mother, but with her kind of condition, I always worried if she would be around to see Parker grow into a young woman. I gently placed my hand on my client's shoulder to tell her we would get through this.

Seeing her sit beside me in dampened spirits made me think of Autumn. That bruise on her arm that I had noticed earlier really pissed me off. She was such a sweet girl, and I hoped like hell that no man was out here abusing her and making her feel less than human.

My mother had a phase where she was being abused, and my brother and I tried to kill the man responsible for her pain. I believed that everyone had to go through and get through shit on their own, but she was my mother, and I would move mountains for that lady. Back in the day, my tempered ways would fly off the hinges when it came to that woman.

So, to find out that a man was putting his hands on her had me in a different headspace, with the only thing on my mind being murder. I don't remember much from the night that my brother and I had finally caught up with the man who was responsible for my mother's pain. Luckily, that was before I had become a lawyer, and our crime of assault never saw the inside of a courtroom.

My brother, on the other hand, was still that same hot head. Growing up, I was the nigga in the hood that could fight and really well. I didn't need a gang or a group a niggas to put a battery in my back to put a nigga down. To find out that my brother had fallen to being in a gang was frustrating, to say the least, but it was a path that he had to walk on his own. To tell the truth, he and I weren't as close as we used to be because of life decisions he had made for himself. One thing that we did come together on was anything involving our mother or our kids.

"Officer Hoover, do you have anything else to add," the judge interrupted my running thoughts. I was sitting in my head when my client needed me the most.

"I do not," the officer removed himself from the stand and exited.

While he was talking, I ended up jotting down some notes. On the criminal side, my client was facing obstruction of property and disturbing the peace. I was glad that when my client did flip out, she kept her hands to herself because that made my fight with her to get full custody of their child with this divorce a bit easier. Once I noticed that the father had a past of drug use, I wasn't worried a bit. This was a clean sweep for me.

I could tell that, more than anything, my client was upset with her actions. I could relate. Allowing someone to get you out of character was a hard pill to swallow, especially when the evidence was tossed into your face. I spent two hours inside the courtroom going back and forth and was happy that things were over. The side sneer that the judge had given me let me know that I had this one in the bag.

I left out of court with my head held high because it was another win under my belt. We had to repeat this again the next day just to hear the judge's ruling this time. That was my last case, so I was excited to leave court. Since my mother was back from vacation, she had fallen back into her routine. She would pick up Parker from basketball practice while I headed to the gym. The drive from the courthouse to the gym was a little way, but my music kept me company.

You told me I could trust you, don't lie
I could really use it
Everybody need love, even niggas like me
You told me I could trust you
And I could really use it

Brent was talking his talk, and I sang along. I was so in tune with the song because, at the end of the day, all a man really wanted was somebody in his corner that he could trust. I ran over this pothole and then sucked my teeth because immediately after, my tire pressure light illuminated on the dashboard. *Fuck,* I lightly mumbled when I realized that something must have been stuck in my tire. I hated inconveniences. This stop to handle this tire would throw me off my workout schedule.

I made a right on Memorial Drive when I realized I wasn't far from Tony's Tire Shop. When I pulled up and exited the car, I inspected the tire and saw that the driver's front side had little to no air. I sighed as I walked to the entrance and let myself into a whole bunch of chaos.

"A new tire for what? I specifically said a used tire."

Even from looking at her from behind, I could tell that the woman raising hell was Autumn. Her petite frame was shapely. The same burgundy pencil skirt she had on earlier had little wrinkles in the back from sitting down and then getting up all day. Her hand was on her hip, and her accent was at an all-time high with her attitude. New York women held a spice to them that was intriguing yet familiar because I was from New Jersey.

"Ma'am, as I explained before, for your Jeep, we don't have used tires; we only have new tires. So, at this point, you can either pay for the tire, or we will put the damaged one back on since you don't have a spare in the trunk. The choice is yours, love."

She let out an annoyed sigh and then pulled her phone from the brown bag hanging from her forearm. Slides were on her tiny feet instead of the brown heels she wore earlier.

"$150 is insane," I heard her mumble as I approached. Tony looked up from his phone, happy to see me.

"Patience, hey buddy. What are you here for?"

"To pay for her tire and a change on one of mine outside."

Autumn quickly looked in my direction, and then a small smile appeared on her face.

"You don't have to do that, Mr. Jacobs."

She responded as I sneakily peered at her phone and saw her transferring money to pay for the tire. From what I could see, she didn't have much in her savings, and the tire price probably would have set her back a bit. Hopefully, she had another account tucked away somewhere. If not, then I knew that the tire cost would be her last until payday in the morning.

"We aren't at work, Autumn. Calling me by my first name will do, and no, I insist."

I quickly handed Tony my card before she could object again.

"Aye, somebody, go outside and change the tire." Tony looked my way, "Do you still have the Mercedes?" He asked.

I nodded my head yes.

"Change the tire on that Mercedes A.S.A.P."

Someone from the back hurried out and did what was asked of him. After charging my credit card, Tony handed it back to me.

"Give them like fifteen minutes, Patience. Mam, your jeep is ready, and they will be pulling it out shortly," he directed the ending of his statement to Autumn.

Tony, more than anybody, knew that although my name was Patience, it was something that I seriously lacked. I had been coming to him for my cars since I moved here for college. He knew the street me. Having Parker changed my life drastically, and I was blessed for that. I looked over to the front and saw that he had made some changes since the last time I was there. A sitting area was right in the front, so I ushered for us to sit. There was an awkward silence.

"Is this why you were late today?" I asked, trying to spark conversation. When I left for court earlier that day, I noticed her car was not in the parking lot.

"Yes, I got good on 285 and realized one of my tires was flat. I don't even know how. The tire pressure wasn't low when I got in from the gym last night."

I was impressed with her going to the gym. Her body looked amazing to me. Being a woman who took pride enough in her body to push herself to workout was a turn-on for me, especially since I was a frequent gym member.

"Is that a problem? Like was it. I'm usually not late or anything. I'm usually—"

She was panicking, and I saw it all over her profile.

"Autumn, you're fine. You're human. It's okay."

Usually, it wouldn't be okay with me, but like I said, I had the illest crush on her since she started working for me. The tenseness seemed to leave her body with my statement. I felt like telling her that she looked pretty today because she really fucking did. Her hair was bone straight and to her shoulders. She always held this natural glow to her. Just when I mustered up the courage to spit it out, Tony interrupted.

"Mam, your car is ready. Yours too, Patience."

We both stood simultaneously, and it seemed she was rushing to get somewhere. She walked toward the front door, and I reached for my arm around her to open it.

"Thank you," she said lowly as I held the door.

Her spring-like scent tickled under my nose as she passed by. I could tell the smell was designer by how it lingered behind her. I knew that she must have fancied the finer things in life, but judging by that bank account, she couldn't afford them.

"Thank you for everything," she turned around and said when we both made it outside.

"See you tomorrow," I called out before getting into my car.

"Yes, early and on time!" She eagerly said before hopping in her Jeep and driving away.

I stood outside my car as I watched until I couldn't see her truck anymore. That bruise on her arm crossed my mind.

"Aye Tony, that lady… what caused her flat, do you know?" I called out as he quickly walked by.

"Looks like somebody slashed her tire, man."

"Thanks," I said right before getting into my car.

It appeared that Autumn had some shit going on with her, and for the life of me, I don't know why I was eager to find out what it was. I was ready to find out more about her. I needed to know who she was outside of work. I quickly hopped in my car and then made my way home. I had a lot of shit going on with my own life, and there I was, trying to pry into someone else's drama. My phone vibrated in my hand, causing me to look down while I waited at the traffic light.

Ma: Where are you?

: Caught a flat on the way home

I quickly texted my mother back before the light turned green. My day moved on a schedule so much that even my mother worried when I would deviate from such. For the rest of the ride home, I drove in silence. I didn't play my music, and regularly, anyone who drove without music or something playing was a serial killer in my mind. However, silence was needed because Autumn was on my mind.

Chapter 4

Lamar Hoover

I sat on my brother's couch, drinking a beer as I thought about where my life now was. When I walked out of the courtroom earlier that day, I first checked my phone. I hated days when I was summoned to testify in court. I saw that I had no texts or missed calls from Autumn. I had driven to her house the night before and punctured one of her tires just enough to cause a slow leak.

I was hopeful that she would give me a call when she was left stranded on the side of the road. The entire day had passed, and my phone didn't ring. I guess she was really cool on my ass. I put the empty Corona bottle down next to the other three empty ones.

As I sat in my brother's dark living room, the light from my phone illuminated the murky quarters. I was on Autumn's Instagram page and saw that she hadn't posted anything. No heartbreaking memes, no pictures of herself, nothing. I only saw that she had taken down the images of her and me. She blocked my regular page, so I was signed into one of my numerous fake pages to spy on her. The light turning on caused me to squint my eyes until my sights adjusted.

"You need to get your life together," Luther said with a bit of disgust.

This was day three of staying with my little brother; every chance he got, he reminded me why he was the favorite in the family. Luther was a realtor, had his own everything, and didn't let the stress of relationships deteriorate what he had going for himself.

I showed repeatedly that I would be a crash-out dummy for someone I loved. Before Autumn, I had almost lost my mind over my high school sweetheart. Once I bounced back from that heartbreak, I met Autumn. I locked my phone when he walked over in my direction.

"What?" he sucked his teeth, "have you been drinking since you've been off?" He asked as he started to pick up the empty beer bottles.

"Yeah," I cracked another bottle open and tossed the cap onto the nearby coffee table.

"This shit ain't healthy dog."

He quickly picked up the top I had just tossed along with the other ones on the table.

"Did you even eat?"

He was nagging and annoying, just like how our mother used to be. I swear I don't blame our dad for leaving because that nagging shit would drive me crazy too.

"I had Zaxbys on my lunch break," I admitted.

He fixed his face like he wanted to say something, but instead, he just gathered up my garbage and headed to the nearby trash can. I unlocked my phone and saw that Autumn had posted on her story. *Finally,* I secretly thought.

I had been stalking her page since she put me out, hoping to get a sign of where her head was. She had this pattern of standing on business and then getting weak in the knees. I was just waiting on the latter.

She had the LED lights I had installed behind the television powered on and set to a soft blue with a candle lit. On the boomerang of what looked like The Blacklist playing on the television, she had the word peace written in big bold letters. She was such a homebody that stuck to the same routine. I used to beg her to try out other shows, but that one was somewhat of a safe haven for her.

If she was serious about being done with me, I wondered when she would have the time to date someone else. A piece of me wondered if she had a man over. That's what females do, leave one and move on to the next. My high school sweetheart had really done a number on me when it came to the cheating shit. When women boasted about dog walking a nigga it was nothing compared to what Alicia had put me through.

When it came to being devious and conniving, she could teach a class on the shit. Just the thought of Autumn possibly doing to me a fraction of what Alicia had made me quickly get on my feet.

"Where are you going?" Luther asked when he saw me jump up from the couch and then grab my keys off the coffee table.

I wore Nike gray sweatpants, a white shirt, and some socks. I slid my bare feet into my Nike slides and grabbed my wallet. I didn't care that I looked crazy; I needed to see who was over there. There was a burning feeling in my gut that her standing firm on being done with me had everything to do with another man.

"I gotta make a move," I quickly spat out.

"Don't do anything stupid, bro."

Being around when I had lost my shit over Alicia, he knew how far I could take things when I felt like my heart was being played with. I ignored his statement as I headed out the door. I pushed my Dodge Durango to limits I hadn't before as I drove to Autumn's place. Just the thought of another man in her presence angered me. Although she was done, I wasn't, and that's all that mattered to me. She was going to fuck around and get somebody killed, thinking that she could just move on from me.

Once I let myself into the complex with the access fob I still had, I parked and then logged into the Ring App that I still had access to. I watched the videos from earlier that day and saw she had come inside alone. She looked drained but yet still so damn pretty. She was naturally pretty, and that was one of the things I loved most about her.

Her big, pouty lips were heart-shaped when her face was resting. When she was angry, those lips would pucker up in disgust over something I had done. I sat in my truck for a while, thinking about many things I had taken for granted. I had watched the video of her entering the house earlier a few more times, and to be honest, I felt like shit. She looked like she had a day, and the stress that coated her profile made me think I needed to find a way to make things right.

Autumn didn't deserve more than half of the shit that I had put her through, but I'm man enough to admit that I was still working through some of my demons that I had from when we first started dating. Instead of handling them, I pushed them to the back burner to give her my full attention. I now realized that it wasn't fair to her.

I should have taken the time to heal myself before even approaching her. I should have put in the work to figure out what triggered me to do half of the shit that I did. She didn't deserve what I assumed to be love. I put my phone in my pocket before exiting the truck. A piece of me wanted to try and get some flowers from somewhere, but it was so late at night. I knocked on the door a few times before ringing the bell. When the blue ring from the ring camera came on, I knew she was looking at me.

"Autumn, open the door," I said in the sweetest tone I could muster.

"Lamar, leave."

I took a deep breath because I felt my temper rising. I couldn't for the life of me understand why she was so stiff on me. Granted, I had put her through a lot over the years, but our history of good didn't outweigh the bad? When the light went off, I pressed the button again.

"What!" She was yelling, and that pissed me off more.

I snatched the camera off the door and then started to walk away.

"Put my camera back."

"Come get it," I calmly said as I returned to the truck.

"You know what? Keep it!" she yelled.

I knew the Wi-Fi connected to the camera couldn't stretch that far. I got into my truck and tossed the camera in the passenger seat before returning to my brother's house. The typical tactics I used to get my woman back weren't working, so I needed to go back to the drawing board and try different strategies.

☙ ☙ ☙ ☙ ☙ ☙

Autumn

I couldn't sleep much after the night I had. I barely slept out of fear that Lamar would kick my door in. With his temper, you really never knew what to expect. Instead of drowning in sorrow, I prepared for work. I had a point to prove to

Patience. I said I would be on time and wanted to be early.

Since it was Friday, I wore a pair of slim-fit jeans, some cheetah flats, and a white blouse. I tossed some loose curls into my hair and then hurried and put my clothes on. I couldn't wait to tell Amani how he had paid for my tire. It was the strangest thing running into him there. I texted her when I got home, but she didn't respond.

Before heading to work, I checked all four tires because Lord knows I didn't need a repeat of yesterday. I felt good riding through the city. The weather was nice enough to have my windows rolled down. Not too much, though, because I didn't want to mess my curls up. I stopped at Starbucks to get coffee for everyone and was still thirty minutes early to work.

I could have everyone's coffee on their desk and start working on Patience's case files early. I unlocked the door and headed to Mr. Jackson's office first since he was closest to the front door.

"I am sooooo sorry!"

I damn near dropped the tray of coffee out my hand when I walked in and saw a woman bent over his desk. His whole ass was out while he was drilling her from behind.

"Autumn, wait," I turned around when I heard Amani's voice.

While Mr. Jackson was pulling up his slacks, Amani fixed her skirt and buttoned her top. She was rushing behind me, I'm sure to explain what I had just walked in on. Personally, I didn't give a damn about what they had going. I cared about catching it and prayed that Mr. Jackson wouldn't fire me for it.

I'm sure he would rather protect his job than mine. That's what I had to learn from being a secretary. It didn't come with the same job security as prior jobs that I had, but it came with peace of mind, and I preferred that over everything.

"Girl, don't tell Mr. Jacobs..." she pleaded.

"Don't tell me what?"

I looked up and saw that Patience was standing in the practice doorway. *Damn, is everyone coming to work early?* I thought to myself as I stared at him. The dip in his thick eyebrows demanded an answer and quickly. His sights shifted between Amani and me.

"Amani misplaced one of your files from the printer, but I found it and will have it on your desk shortly. Coffee?" I asked as I held the tray out.

I figured that since that was something she would typically do, no repercussions would come from it. Patience took a coffee from the tray and sniffed the air before walking into his office. He was doing exactly what I had done when I walked in. The air did have this sex smell to it, but I guess because of the cool temperature, it wasn't as noticeable.

When he closed his office door, I put the coffee on the corner of my desk.

"Girl, what are you thinking?" I blurted out because I couldn't contain my shock any longer.

"Listen, we've been dating a little since I started," she explained.

"Autumn, a word?" Mr. Jackson was standing in the doorway of his office.

I blew out a sharp breath because, like I had told Amani, I needed this job, and if it was a me or her thing, then I had to choose me.

She still lived at home with her parents; I know she had no bills. One wouldn't have thought they would have seen what I had just done judging by Mr. Jackson's appearance. Like Patience, he was always dapper on the regular and appeared to be in place. I almost forgot that he was just balls deep in my best friend.

After his statement, he walked back into his office as if talking with him wasn't much of a decision. I ice-grilled Amani on the way toward his office. I walked in and then closed the door behind me. Whenever I was called into someone's office, I shut the door behind me to give them the respect and privacy I felt they needed. He took a seat behind his desk before he spoke.

"I wanted to apologize for what you walked in on."

"I didn't walk in on anything," I quickly responded.

I loved this job and needed him to understand that whatever he and Amani had going on was none of my business. He tapped the pen in his hand on the desk and then gave me a smirk.

"Understood," he said calmly.

"Is there anything else?" I asked.

When he shook his head, I let myself out.

There was steady silence in the front of the lobby as Amani and I sat at our desks. The other two attorneys came in, and I welcomed them to the coffee I had brought. As I sat in silence, I started to piece together little pieces, and everything started to make sense to me. The day prior, Amani was all cheesy on her phone, and I'm sure it was to talk to him.

Usually, when I call Amani, she answers, so the night before, without getting a text back, made sense. I could feel her eyes looking at me with worry, so I decided to break some of the tension.

"You was bent over the desk like a little whore. It's very much given porn," I whispered.

She spit out her orange juice in a giggle.

"Girl," she managed to get out in between her laughing. She grabbed a nearby napkin off her desk and cleaned the orange juice.

"I feel better now that you know," she admitted.

"We gotta go out for drinks because there's some things I need to tell you too," I said.

In between being unable to sleep the night before because I was worried about Lamar returning, Patience was also on my mind. Being in his presence screamed, being in the presence of a protector, and I loved that. The way he carried himself gave me this feeling that as long as I was with him, I would be okay.

"I'm out the door, ladies," he said in an even tone, breezing past Amani and me with his briefcase in tow.

I knew that the verdict for this divorce and custody case he had going on for the past couple of months was expected to be in today. I hoped that everything worked out in his favor.

"Good luck," I called out when he approached the door.

He turned around and then gave me a wink before saying thanks.

"What was that about?" Amani asked with a sly look on her face.

"Girl, I'll tell you about it later."

The corners of my mouth turned upward as I thought about the fine man who had just walked out of the door.

Chapter 5

Patience

"The defendant is subject to pay $497 biweekly for the child on the case, and full custody is granted to the mother…"

The judge went on to state that in the state of Georgia, my client and her ex were officially divorced. The happiness across my client's face couldn't be hidden even if she tried.

"I told you we got this," I said with a smile.

This was my last case for the day, and I was ending it with a win. I walked out of the courtroom side by side with my client. I reminded her to make her other court date, which was a month out. I told her that I would text and check on her. I'm sure that, in that case, she would be given anger management.

I powered my phone back on while I was making my exit.

Autumn McKinley: Did you win your case?

I involuntarily smiled when I read Autumn's text.

: I did

I texted her back quickly as I walked across the parking lot to my car. Seeing those three dots pop up while she was typing gave me this funny feeling in my stomach.

Autumn McKinley: Congratulations. Can I take you out to celebrate? Something small, I promise. Plus, I feel the need to repay you for my tire.

I checked the watch on my wrist and saw it was five in the afternoon. Usually, I would have gone to the gym, but the hour and a half that I usually dedicated to my body could be missed today if that meant that I could spend some time with Autumn.

: that's cool. What you got in mind?

I waited as the three bubbles showed on our text thread, which meant she was responding. She shot me an address, and I quickly clicked on it so my GPS could navigate me there. The drive there wasn't long. One thing I loved about the city: if your route had no traffic, you could get there in less than twenty minutes. I don't know if she had thought of this spot last minute or had been thinking about it all day.

Whatever the reason, I was grateful because I was hungry, and I loved Mexican food. *Tacos and Tequila,* I read in my head and entered the parking lot behind the establishment. I had heard about it all over social media but didn't have time to go.

Matthew

I looked down and saw that Matt was calling me.

"Hello?" I answered as I texted Autumn to let her know I was there.

"Congrats on your win, bro. Miss the gym, let's go for drinks."

"Thanks. I think I'm kinda doing that right now."

"With who?" His tone was curious because, being my day one, he would be the first to know if I was dating somebody.

Truth is, I didn't know what this was. Autumn could simply be thanking me for that tire, or she could have a genuine interest in me how I do in her.

Autumn McKinley: Come inside. I'll be waiting for you.

"Uhh, ima tell you later, bro. I gotta go."

"Ahh, this muthafucka done went off and got himself a bitch," I heard him laugh just before he ended the line.

I exited the car, making sure that my suit was intact before I walked into the establishment.

"Hey you, she's ready to seat us," Autumn said excitedly.

"Hey," I calmly responded, involuntarily smiling at how excited she seemed to see me. I caught myself about to lean in for a friendly hug, but I wasn't sure we were there yet.

As we walked behind the waitress to our seats, I had to check myself mentally. I was intrigued by this woman, and I didn't want that to turn into a delusion that she felt the same way. Tonight will tell for sure.

"Your server will be with you shortly, okay?" The woman said to us as she placed menus down at our table.

I quickly watched Autumn pull her chair out before I could get around to it. I could tell that she likely had a past with men who proved that chivalry was dead. I still opened doors for women, pulled out chairs, and came with random flowers. I don't see how any of these dudes were getting coochie now of days. Crazy enough, my gentlemanly ways were probably my downfall as well.

That's undoubtedly one of the reasons that when I did get a woman who I thought was of substance, I would get dog-walked and taken advantage of.

"Thank you for my tire," Autumn broke me from my thoughts.

"Like I told you yesterday, it's really nothing."

There was a silence between us as she looked through her menu.

"I'm Pablo. I'll be your waiter today. Are you guys ready?"

"Just give us a minute," I said when I realized Autumn was still flipping the menu and checking out both sides.

"I'll be back," he responded before scurrying away.

There was another moment of silence as she continued to look over the menu.

"I want to try these drinks I saw all over Instagram. They come three in one," she turned the menu to show me what she was talking about.

I already knew what I wanted when I first glanced at the menu. I was starving but didn't want to pig out since I would miss a day at the gym.

"I saw those on Instagram too. I think it's called the flight or something like that," I admitted.

"So you're gonna get one with me?" She showed off her pearly whites after her statement.

"I'll have one drink, but not that because it comes with three. I still have to drive home."

I had to drive through the city to get home, and the last thing I needed was to get pulled over.

"Loosen your tie some, Attorney Jacobs. This is a celebration. I know I need the damn drinks," she admitted as she raised her hand for the waiter, that had briefly introduced himself and then walked away to give us more time to look at the menu.

While she ordered her food, I did undo my tie because I was, in fact, dressed in a full suit. I ordered myself a steak quesadilla and one margarita. She was right. We were celebrating, and although I didn't drink unless it was the weekend, I deserved this one.

"There we go now he looks relaxed," she said with a smile once the tie around my neck was loose and my dress shirt was unbuttoned from around my Adam's apple.

It was nice seeing her outside of the work element. She probably felt the same toward me, especially since I kept things short, sweet, and professional inside those doors. Her cheetah print blouse had both arms exposed, and the bruise was as clear as day. It was in that dark purple healing stage. The waiter came and dropped our drinks down, and before he could make his exit, she grabbed one of her drinks and started to down it.

Intrigued, I blinked my eyes a few times and then raised my thick eyebrows at her actions. I was a party promoter in high school and college, so I could drink like a sailor. Again, that was another part of my life, and I retired when Parker was born. My friends even got me a hat that said *retired party promoter* because when I was doing it, I was doing it big.

"The bruise is from my ex."

She had caught me off guard entirely with her comment.

"I saw you looking, and that isn't the first time, so I finally decided to address it," she added.

I felt like shit for making my staring be the reason she felt the need to come clean with her secrets.

"I'm sorry," I really was.

"For what? He did me wrong for years, and I finally have had enough."

She grabbed her second drink and started sipping on that one.

"That's good for you then. There's no real love in someone who breaks your heart repeatedly and watches you pick up the pieces," I said before taking a sip of my water.

Now, with it confirmed that she was a victim of domestic violence, I really felt for her. She had started telling me about the ex-boyfriend she had met in college, which had changed her life for the worse. In between her talking, the waiter brought our food. I started to eat and drink as I listened.

"Now, what's your story?" She said at the end of her long speech.

I couldn't just reciprocate how she had because I had multiple women over the years, and there was way more to tell than dealing with one person who had done me wrong, so I kept things short and sweet. I told her I had a fantastic daughter and was upfront about my living arrangement.

"I think that's sweet that you live with your mother to look after her."

Most women didn't see it that way, so I appreciated that she did. Her phone started ringing, and then she placed it face down on the table. Once she did, I thanked her.

"Thank you."

I noted her placing her phone down, and everything in me wanted to know who had called her, but it wasn't my place to ask. I could feel myself genuinely interested in her, and I was curious to know who was interrupting *our* time.

Since she seemed unbothered by it, I would also have to be. She continued with the conversation as if nothing happened.

"And being a single dad must not be easy," she said after chewing some of her food.

She had no idea, but I was managing, and according to my friends, I was doing the damn thing even if, at most times, I didn't feel that way. I knew I was a good dad, but with so much on my plate at times, I felt like I was doing a disservice to Parker.

At times, I felt like I worked too much or wasn't as present as I should have been, but I knew that working had to come high on my priority list for her to get a fraction of the nice things she had. The only thing I could do was raise her to the best of my ability, and I hope that when she's older, she will feel the same way as my boys do.

"It has its challenges. Do you have any?"

She had no pictures on her desk, so I assumed she didn't. Her eyes went dark, and I regretted asking the question because it seemed I had changed her mood.

"No, but I would love to have one someday."

There was an awkward silence after her statement, so I changed the subject and dug into her background. She was surprised when she learned that I was originally from New Jersey. She admitted that my accent gave off northerner, but she couldn't pinpoint exactly where. She got good into her third drink when I heard a little slur in her words.

If her three drinks were anything as strong as my one, then I knew that in no time, she would be tore up. Judging by how her volume in tone had raised I could tell that the drinks were finally sneaking up on her. We both had finished our food, and she was throwing back the last bit of her drink when the bill came. I quickly snatched it up and handed the waiter one of my credit cards.

"I said it was on me, Patience."

"I heard you when you said it, and I say it's on me."

Her eyes were glossy, and I knew I wouldn't let her drive home like that. I could tell she didn't get out much by how she downed her drinks. Either that or this breakup she was going through had her all messed up. The waiter brought my card back, and when he did, I pulled out the chair for Autumn.

"Such a gentleman, thank you," she said with a smile.

"I honestly feel like you are too wasted to drive yourself home. Do you want me to put you in an Uber or take you? There's no work tomorrow, so you can always come back for your jeep."

"You can take me. Where did you park?"

"This way," I started to walk toward the back of the parking lot, and like a child, I felt her reach for my hand.

Her small palm filled the inside of my hand, and I smiled.

"Just so I won't fall, you know," she casually said.

"Yeah, just so you won't fall," I chuckled.

If I was unsure if she was feeling me before, then that confirmed it. She had this innocent way of flirting that let me know she had only dealt with one man when it came to dating as an adult.

I helped her get into the car and waited for her to get comfortable before closing the door. When I got into the driver's seat, I waited for her to put her address on my phone so that I could use the GPS.

'Cause when we hurt each other we come back to
help each other heal
You say I'm crazy, but at least you know my love is
real
But shit, you crazy too, and that's why they say love
is hell

"And it's forever, so I hope you never up and bail, and if you ever left me for someone, you gon' get someone killed," she was singing with her eyes closed.

For a moment, I felt like I was intruding on a personal moment. Autumn was relating to Joyner Lucas' song in a way I couldn't. I didn't play those toxic games, and the person had to go as soon as they ever came. She was, in fact, just getting out of a relationship, and then I realized that pursuing her would be a dangerous game. Her heart was still so fragile, and although I knew that I would safeguard it, I didn't need the baggage that I knew she would surely come with.

"Hey, pretty girl, where's your fob for the gate."

She had fallen asleep on the ride, and although we weren't in the car for long, I knew the drinks she consumed had much to do with that.

"Hey," I nudged her, "how do we get in your gate beautiful?"

She pulled her keys out of her purse and held her hand up.

The gate had opened for us. I followed the GPS down to her apartment.

"So you think I'm beautiful?" She asked once I parked outside of her building.

"I think you know that, but you must have forgotten. I didn't like how your story was going, so I'm here to fix it."

I was boldly stating that my interest in her was here. Whatever she said next would let me know if I should fall back and proceed cautiously.

"Are you now?"

She leaned over the middle console and then kissed my cheek. Although I was the darkest shade of brown, I knew that I had to be blushing like a muthafucka.

"Goodnight, Mr. Jacobs."

She gathered her bag and then exited my car. I sat parked and waited for her to enter her apartment before I pulled off. Her house was ten minutes from my house, and I knew the circumstances could benefit me in the future.

⁂ ⁂ ⁂ ⁂ ⁂ ⁂

Lamar

With my headlights turned out, I watched as the midnight blue Mercedes exited Autumn's complex. I was still on duty and had just dropped an inmate off at the county. After that task, my travels landed me right outside of her complex. I figured I would take another crack at getting her back, especially since my calls about an hour ago went unanswered.

I was about to drive in and pay her a visit when I saw the car with her on the passenger side slowly cruise past me. When the driver got to the corner and made a left without a signal, I turned on my headlights, drove quickly down the street, and made the same left he had. I hit my lights and sirens and then waited for him to pull over so that I could pull behind him.

The driver pulled over and then turned his engine off. I ran his plates while he was waiting for me to engage and saw that the vehicle was registered to Patience Jacobs. When I exited the vehicle, I slowly strolled over to the car. A ploy I did to make the driver nervous.

If they had anything to hide, this, in fact, worked. While passing, I lightly placed my hand on the trunk of the vehicle, something I had learned in police training that never left me. We did that to check for movement inside the trunk. I realized how important that was because I worked in Atlanta, and human trafficking was at an all-time high.

"Do you know why I pulled you over?" I led with the statement that we all led with.

When I saw who I was addressing, I recognized him. I had seen him earlier that week when I was summoned to court to testify. He looked down at my name badge before responding.

"I do not. Please inform me."

He had both his hands on the steering wheel. I could tell that he either had a run-in with the police before or that his occupation as a lawyer had taught him the proper way to conduct himself in the presence of law enforcement.

"You turned without a signal," I knew he wasn't one of the ones I could play with.

"I did. I apologize for that. I'm just trying to get home," Patience squinted his eyes as he looked at me intensely. I assume he was trying to remember exactly where he had seen me. "I know you," he admitted.

"I was in court yesterday on one of your cases. How did it go?"

I was intrigued to know. I hated getting called to testify, but I knew the kid would have been better off with his mother.

"My client won," he said with pride.

"That's good. The kid would be better off with the mom between you and me anyway." I had busted the dad on numerous petty accounts before.

"Aye, listen, ima let you go with a warning."

"Preciate it," he thanked me.

As I walked back to my squad car, a piece of me wanted to ask where he was coming from, but my obsession and problem was with Autumn, not him. As I watched him start his car and then drive off, a piece of me became jealous of the possibility of her moving on.

Chapter 6

Patience

When I got in the night before, I was so drained that I peeled off my clothes and got straight into bed. The morning sun was peeking through my blinds, and I realized I didn't know what time it was. I snatched my phone off the charger and saw it was ten in the morning. Usually, I don't sleep in this late, but I guess I need the rest. I had no text messages from Autumn, so I figured she was sleeping later than I was. She did have more drinks than I did.

I sniffed the air because I smelled sausage and eggs. My mother must have been cooking, and like a kid, I hopped out of bed and then tossed on some basketball shorts before heading to the kitchen. I rubbed my hands across my bare chest as I made my way.

"Oh, now he wakes up. You must have smelt the food, huh?"

When I rounded the corner like I had predicted, I saw my mother in the kitchen. The simple fact that she knew that I was coming before even seeing me was that mother shit that she will always have instilled in her.

"Pumpkin wanted some breakfast, so here you're lucky."

She handed me a plate as soon as I entered the kitchen.

"Thank you."

I glanced into the dining room and didn't see Parker sitting at the table.

"Where is she?" I asked.

"She scarfed that food down and then ran downstairs to play with Jackie's granddaughter."

My mother made friends everywhere she went, so when we moved into this place, she quickly befriended every neighbor and even people in the management office.

I placed my plate on the island and sat at one of the tall barstools. It was rare when Parker got a Saturday that didn't revolve around basketball, so I was glad that she had the chance to still be a kid. That was all thanks to my mother. She knew all of the neighbors and had so many friends and extended family members from all of the traveling that she had done.

It was easy to love someone like my mother because she was kind-hearted and genuine. After loving my mother, all her friends fell in love with Parker.

"So who is she?"

"Hmm?"

I let a little bit of egg fall out of my mouth as I responded to my mother. She grabbed a towel from the handle on the stainless steel stove and dried her hands before repeating herself.

"Who is she?"

She had just finished washing dishes and stood in front of me with bold eyes, waiting for a response.

"Pshh, what are you talking about, woman?" I tried to joke and laugh.

"Boy, you came in late last night, and I figured you weren't at anybody's gym because I didn't hear the water running last night. Now you're either dirty as hell or seeing a woman."

I couldn't stop the corners of my mouth from turning upward if I tried. Nothing could get past my mother. I enjoyed the night before with Autumn and honestly wanted to pick my mother's brain about her situation.

"This woman, Autumn, took me out to celebrate me winning that case."

"Autumn, that works for you?"

I shook my head up and down as I gathered some more scrambled eggs onto my fork before taking a bite.

"You don't think that will be kind of messy?"

A work romance was something I had never thought I would entertain, but it was something about Autumn that made me want to try it.

"I don't think so. Autumn's very professional like me, and I think we can maintain that professionalism inside that building. Her situation with her ex is messy," I openly admitted.

My mother raised her eyebrow and then sat on the other end of the island.

"What do you mean?" she asked.

I had reiterated things to my mother exactly how Autumn had explained things to me the night before.

"Mmm," was what she muttered once I had finished telling her the story that was said to me.

"Loving on a woman like her that has been through so much is a little different. You need to love her in her love language and be mindful of her heart. It's in a fragile position right now, and if you are going to pursue that woman, you need to always have that in the front of your mind."

"It's already there," I gave her a wink before picking up my empty plate and setting it in the sink.

My mother was a victim of domestic violence, so I knew that she could probably relate to Autumn in ways that I couldn't.

"Boy, wash your dish. I know you just saw me clean all of those."

She threw the towel in her hands at my back, and it landed on my shoulder. I chuckled before quickly washing the plate and fork.

"Does she have any children?"

The question was so random that I had forgotten that we were still talking about Autumn.

"Nope, it's just her."

"Okay, well, be conscious that you do have one. I understand wanting to love Autumn because she deserves love just like any other woman, but don't let her personal life, don't let her past, mess up what you got going for yourself."

I took heed of everything she said because she had a front-row seat to how my marriage could have taken everything from me. Emotionally, it drained me to the point where I couldn't even be there the way I would have liked for Parker.

Mentally I was fucked up, and my mother had stepped up without complaining or throwing the shit in my face. I promised myself that I would never allow anyone to take me back to that dark place.

"I know," I finally managed to say, "what's on the agenda for today?"

"Well, pumpkin and I are going to volunteer at the road race. You can do whatever you please. Go spend time with ya lady friend or Matthew's crazy ass."

She reminded me that I had to call Matt back.

"Okay, well, I'll find some business for the day."

"You do that," she stood and went to her room.

When I returned to my room, I saw that I had a text from Autumn telling me good morning, and she was letting me know that she had picked up her car from the restaurant parking lot. I also received a text message from Matthew asking how my night had gone.

I didn't even realize that I had sat and talked for my mother as long as I did until I noticed my phone said it was close to noon. I knew Matthew would be up because he was an early bird like me.

"What's the word?" He answered on the second ring.

"Man ain't shit for real."

"Ahh ahh, what the bitches be saying? Umm na, I need the tea."

I busted out laughing because Matthew was the most unserious person I knew.

"It's Patience on the phone, damn woman. You gone clock every muthafucking move of mine."

I heard Matthew say away from the phone.

"Tina said what's up bro," he returned to the phone and said.

"Tell sis I said what's good."

Tina and Matthew had been dating since college. His ass just came back from a week's vacation at Grand Turks because he had finally buckled down and asked her to marry him.

"Now, back to you, who you had drinks with last night?"

I paused momentarily because I second-guessed if I should say exactly who I had spent my evening with. We did, in fact, work together. I knew Matt was my best friend, but I didn't want to do or say anything that would have Autumn looked at a certain way.

"Spit it out, bruh."

"Me and Autumn went out for drinks."

It sounded like his ass had dropped the phone.

"Naaaaaa, Autumn, we work with?" I could hear him walking around the house, and when I heard a couple of doors close, I knew he was trying to create some distance between him and Tina.

"That's the only Autumn that I know."

"You listening to me."

His whispering had me pushing the phone further into my ear.

"Yeah," I whispered back.

It was a habit I had when people started that whispering shit.

"I fuck with Amani."

"What!" I yelled out.

"Shh shh yeah on some sneaky link low-key shit."

I shook my head because this man just asked another woman to marry him. Matthew has always been an erratic decision-maker, and he has been that way since college. He didn't view marriage how I did because if he did, the opportunity to have a side bitch would have been non existing.

"Bro, you fucking up."

I was into the fashion of calling a spade a spade. Tina and Matthew had their fair share of rough times, but if he wasn't her person, he was better off letting her go find who was.

"I mean, I knowww," he dragged.

Matthew was the kind of person who got emotionally invested in everything he did. He would pour his emotions into the cases he took and fall hard for whoever he messed with.

"You about to marry this woman. You need to nip that shit with Amani in the bud."

"I kinda love them both," he admitted.

I slapped my hand on my forehead like the problem was mine. Truth be told, I never liked Tina for real, but no woman deserves to be cheated on.

"Well, you have a decision to make, brother."

The sigh that escaped Matt's mouth told me he was going through it. He did the shit to himself, though.

"I know, I'm gonna figure something out. But hey, you and Autumn? That's the end game, kid."

I wished like hell it was because, honestly, I was tired of going through it with women.

"We gone see."

"Ahh, kill all that we gone see shit. I always know. That baby mama of yours, I told you hell no, and that wife of yours, I told you to run away when the first wedding was canceled due to Covid. That was your sign from God, but noooo, you just had to hop that old-ass wooden broom. Listen to ya, boy, for once."

Matthew did have a point. He had openly expressed his opinions on my past relationships, and I ignored him every single time. I wanted to take my time with Autumn, though, especially with a past like hers.

"This stays between us, though don't get to work and hinting off that you know she and I are talking."

"You're my boy. You know I got you."

He always did, though. When I first took custody of Parker, he was right by my side. He was right by my side when I was going through my divorce. He was fucked up when it came to committing to women, but he was a damn good friend.

My phone vibrating caused me to put Matthew on speakerphone to check my text messages.

Autumn McKinley: I bet you're busy with baby girl. If not, it would be nice to see you today.

"Bet," I said out loud, not meaning to.

"Huh?" Matthew asked confusedly.

"Autumn wants to hang out today."

"Yeah, bro, do that. Who knows, maybe you might get lucky."

Getting my rocks off was the last thing on my mind. I wanted to take my time with Autumn. I tried to be delicate with her because she deserved that.

"I ain't even on that. Let me call you back, though, bro."

I didn't know what Autumn had in mind for the day, but I wasn't about to pass up a chance to see her.

"Okay, cool."

Matthew ended the line just as I was texting Autumn back.

: What did you have in mind?

She texted back damn near instantly.

Autumn McKinley: a calm evening at my place?

I wanted to take her out because I didn't want her to feel as if our being inside had to be a thing. Still, I completely understood not wanting to go out if you thought your funds weren't intact or weren't in the mood for it.

: getting ready now

She texted me back a smiley face that made me smile.

"Daddy, we are leaving," I looked up from my phone and saw Parker standing in my doorway.

"Okay, have fun with Grandma."

"Let's go, Pumpkin," my mother appeared in the doorway behind Parker, "be careful and enjoy your day," she directed the later statement toward me.

My mother wasn't the *I love you* kind of parent. She loved different. I knew she loved my brother and me with everything in her, but she didn't openly express it. On the other hand, I made sure that I reminded Parker of my love for her every chance I got. Since I didn't tell her when she said bye, I texted her that I loved her before I decided to get ready to go to Autumn's place. I had the address in my maps from the night prior, so after getting myself together, I intended to head her way.

⁂ ⁂ ⁂ ⁂ ⁂ ⁂

Autumn

Nerves started to take over me as I waited for Patience to arrive. When I woke up earlier that day, I had a slight hangover, but that was nothing that some Tylenol and breakfast didn't fix. After getting my car from the Tacos and Tequila parking lot, I went to Walmart for another ring camera. Being a single female and living alone, the new camera was mandatory.

I bypassed the hassle of installing it when I saw that Walmart sold a security case. I wouldn't have the problem of Lamar snatching it off my door again because it would damn near be mounted to my front door.

"So, are you going to cook or order food?" I heard Amani yell into the phone.

I had her on speaker while I was tidying up. I second-guessed us kicking it at my place with Lamar being so unpredictable, but with the anniversary of his mom's passing today, I figured that he would be tied up with his brother and that the last thing on his mind would be me.

"I think I'm going to order something when he gets here because I don't know what he likes to eat."

"Okay. Do you look decent?"

I looked down at my pajama set and figured it was cool since we would be inside.

"I think I'm fine. I'm wearing my brown silk pajama set. The shorts with the top."

"Okay, that's fancy. Are you guys doing wine or what?"

I looked at my wine rack and saw that I had a few options.

"Wine because I already have it here."

"Good…"

Amani seemed distracted, and I couldn't put my finger on why.

"So he is alive, hmph," she grunted.

"Huh?" I asked as I lit a candle to give my straightening-up session the final touch.

"Matthew's ass. He has been missing since he's been back from vacation but has the nerve to just text me like he needs to talk to me."

"Mmm," I openly showed my disdain.

We had been on the phone all morning, and she had been complaining about him. I smelled shit in the air, and I wasted no time letting her know that. The way she explained it was that he had come on the scene with the proposition of sex. Being that I knew Amani was a little nympho, I knew that with a man like Mr. Jackson, she probably wouldn't pass up the opportunity.

Me on the other hand, I wanted a man to approach me like the lady that I was. I didn't want sex to be at the forefront of his mind when it came to me.

"Mm, what?" Amani asked. I could tell that she was annoyed by her tone.

"You deserve better."

We had switched places. Now, I was the one reminding her of her self-worth and what she should and shouldn't take. Amani was one of the reasons that I finally stood up for myself, so I'll be damned if I would allow her to be weak in the knees in front of me.

"I know. I'm done with him."

Her tone sounded unsure, but I took what she said at face value.

Patience: what's the code to get in?

"Shit, he's here," I mumbled once I read my text.

: press 302

I quickly texted him back.

"Hold on," I quickly told Amani once my cell phone rang.

After pressing the button to let Patience in, I clicked back over to Amani.

"Hello?" I was pacing around my living room. My eyes scanned everything to make sure that nothing was out of place.

"Spray some of that Gucci in the air and shimmy in it. You about to get some action, Ms. McKinley."

"Shut upppp," I dragged the ending of my statement and rushed into my bedroom.

Guilty Gucci was too damn expensive to shimmy in a damn thing. After spraying my wrist and then my ankles, I heard a knock on my door. My new ring bell went off after the knock.

"I gotta go."

"Have fun for the both of us," Amani chuckled before ending the line.

I placed my phone down on the side of the couch as I went to the front door.

"Hey you," I cooed once I saw Patience's fine ass standing on my Don't Kill My Vibe doormat, "are these for me?" I said in a giddy tone when I realized that he had a bouquet of roses in his hand.

"They are," he confirmed.

I stepped to the side to allow him into my home. Once he was in, I quickly glanced around the parking lot. When I didn't see a cop car or Lamar's Durango, I immediately shut the door and locked it. When I turned around, Patience handed me the roses. It was nice to see him dressed in regular clothes. If I had a feeling that he worked out before, it was confirmed by how his white shirt hugged his bicep.

"You do shoes on or off?"

He was still standing in my foyer while I was near the kitchen.

"It doesn't matter."

I didn't have a set-in-stone rule regarding footwear in my house, but I was pleased when I saw him slide off his Yeezy sneakers and leave them at the door.

I sat the bouquet of roses down on the counter and tried to get myself a vase from the top shelf. His cologne is what told me that he was invading my space.

"Let me help you."

He reached around me and got the vase I was reaching for. After he sat it on the counter, he backed up to give me my space. Everything about this man was a turn-on. It was the way he could do both. I saw him in a suit daily, but the way he was dressed before me, I could tell this was his actual element. The distressed jeans he wore paired well with the plain white t-shirt he had on.

"What?" he asked.

The smirk he wore let me know that he could tell that I was staring at him. He had caught me red-handedly. Today, his bushy brows didn't look so mean. This man had so much sex appeal that my kitty was begging for him to sit me on the counter and take me to Pound Town. He looked like he would just talk you through it, and I swear I wanted to find out if my assumptions were valid.

"You look nice," I admitted as I started to prep the roses to go into the vase.

There was a single white rose in the middle of the bouquet that I hadn't noticed before, "did they make a mistake?" I asked, referring to the one different rose in the bundle.

"Na, that was a special request. One white rose to represent new beginnings for you, love."

My eyes watered because the gesture was sweet as hell. The week felt like it had been whooping my ass since I decided to be single.

"Thank you," I damn near choked out.

"Let them out. It's okay to cry. You gotta release all that hurt, love."

When he wrapped his strong chocolate arms around me, I was involuntarily crying like a baby.

"Shh shh," he said lowly as he rubbed the lower of my back.

The last thing I wanted to do was be so vulnerable around the presence of this man, but he made it so easy for me to embrace the softest sides of myself while around him.

"You are strong, you are worthy, you are the shit, love."

He was feeding my spirit, and honestly, I needed it. Growing up, I never had someone there to do that, and when I felt like everything around me was crumbling, his words of affirmation built me up. I wanted to personally thank whoever had raised this man because he walked in the spirit of a good upbringing.

We stood in my kitchen for a good ten minutes. Without complaining, Patience held me in his embrace for the whole ten. When my back stopped heaving up and down, he finally spoke.

"You got it together? You got that shit out?" he asked.

"Mmmhmm," I pulled away from his embrace, and when I did, he wiped the trail of tears I had left behind.

I stared into his deep brown eyes briefly, and I could see his pupils soften as he looked at me. I didn't know what I had done to deserve to be in his presence, but I was thankful. Without meaning to, I leaned in for a kiss. When our lips touched, my peach jumped, anticipating him touching it. Our tongues intertwined as we passionately kissed.

When our quick, steamy session ended, he had tapped my lips and then my forehead. Those were always sweet to me. I was a sucker for forehead kisses. It was a small, wholesome sentiment of how the other person cared for you.

"Finish putting your little flowers together."

He stood back in my kitchen doorway as if nothing had happened. I gathered the flowers individually and then snipped the end of each stem at an angle. Our interactions and even the kiss felt so natural, as if we had been doing it forever. He made it so easy to be around him.

"Did you eat lunch already?" he asked.

"No, I was kind of waiting for you so that I could order something for us. What do you have a taste for?"

I placed the flowers into the vase while waiting for his response. When he took too long to respond, I turned around to see him looking me up and down. There was a lust in his eyes that made me instantly wet the silk material of my pajama pants.

"Chinese," he finally answered.

I'm sure my cheeks blushed as I smirked before turning away. I picked up the vase and led the way to my living room.

The beautiful flowers would look perfect on my coffee table. I grabbed my phone from the edge of the couch and sat on the chair.

"Come sit. What do you want from the Chinese?"

He sat beside me and then twisted his face up in thought.

"A General Tso chicken combo is cool."

On the Doordash app, I ordered some food for us. The entire apartment was silent, and I couldn't stand when things were quiet.

"Wine?" I asked.

I almost forgotten that I had a pretty good selection.

"Yeah, that's cool."

As I walked over to my wine rack to grab a bottle and into the kitchen, I could feel his eyes following me. I grabbed two wine glasses from my upper cabinet and then filled them with ice from the ice maker on my counter. Once the two cups were filled, I put the bottle of Blueberry XXL under my arm and then put the two glasses into my hand.

When he saw me balancing everything, he stood to help me.

"I got it," I assured as I walked over.

I placed the glasses down onto the marble coasters on the grey coffee table in the center of my living room. I let Patience do the honors of opening the bottle and then filling our glasses.

While he did that, I grabbed the television remote and pressed the blue button in the center.

"Open Netflix," I spoke clearly.

The app opened on the television in front of us, and I clicked away to find something to watch.

"Toss on *The Blacklist*," he said when I quickly tried to rush past my recently watched.

I didn't want him to see that I had a thread of hopeless romantic shows like *Love is Blind* in my watch history. The truth is that I am a hopeless romantic and always have been. That's another reason why I had this habit of dealing with so much bullshit.

"You watch this?" I asked with excitement.

Lamar hated it whenever I put it on.

"Yeah, Red is the shit."

I figured he must have watched the whole show because he didn't complain when I picked up where I left off with the last episode. We were a good episode and a half in when the food arrived. I placed the bag on the coffee table and started dividing the food.

He looked over at my dining room as if we were supposed to sit at the table to eat our food. Truth be told, I only got the set for show. Many times, I ate meals right in my living room or in the bedroom. I could probably count how many times I sat at that table to eat a meal.

"You want to eat at the table?" I finally asked.

"Na, here is cool."

I handed him his platter and sat straight up on the couch to eat mine. We sat there engaged in the show while we ate. He sat his platter on the table in front of us and then leaned off the couch a bit to get something out of his pocket.

When he looked at the phone screen, he politely asked if I could pause the television. Knowing that he was a busy man and the call could have been work-related, I paused the TV and waited for him to finish with his call.

"Yes, little girl," he answered.

The way he held the phone in front of his face, I knew it was a FaceTime call.

"Daddy, Grandma, and I are back from the racetrack. Where are you?"

His daughter had this little rasp to her adorable tone.

"At a friend's house."

"You don't have any friends besides Uncle Matt."

I covered my mouth to chuckle when he looked my way with a playful raised eyebrow, and I laughed harder.

"I do so have friends. Parker enjoy not having basketball today because tomorrow we have practice early. I will see you when I get in."

"Mmhmm, bye daddy."

I heard her hang up, and then I let my laugh loose.

"So you don't have any friends, Mr. Jacobs?" I playfully asked.

"According to my daughter, I guess not."

"So I'm your friend, Mr. Jacobs?"

His dark brown eyes rolled over in my direction, and for a minute, I could have sworn that he was blushing. A red undertone hit those dark-colored cheeks, and I had to smile at his bashful state.

"I'm trying to make you more than my friend Ms. McKinley."

His high cheekbones rose with his smile.

"Mmm," I wiped my hands on the napkin beside me and placed my platter on the coffee table beside his.

"What you doing?" He asked once I straddled him.

I knew what I wasn't going to do was stop myself from doing anything that didn't feel natural. Being around Patience just felt so right. We meshed well, and I was so sexually attracted to him that I couldn't stop myself from letting lust consume me. When I felt him brick up beneath me, I smirked.

"If not just your friend, then what?" I asked before kissing his neck.

"Sss," he hissed, "I want you to be mine."

Since crossing the line between employer and employee, I didn't know I would be walking into a newfound commitment. A piece of me wanted to run for the hills because things seemed to be moving quickly. I had been working there for two years, but besides our most recent actions, I never would have thought that he was interested in me.

"How do you know you want me though? You could just want something from me."

I was rusty with this dating shit, and I'm sure that it showed. Patience was an established man, so I knew he wasn't seeking stability. The only thing that came to mind was something sexual. Like a baby, he placed his strong hands under my arms and lifted me from him. He sat me beside him on the couch.

"I still remember the day you came in for your interview. You were nervous. Like twiddling thumbs, nervous. You wore these nude stockings under your black skirt, and there was a run in the right leg of the back part. I don't think you noticed because you were probably moving so fast, trying to get ready that morning. You wore your hair in a sleek bun to the back. It showed off your face fully. You couldn't make eye contact with Matt or me, but you still held some confidence. With nerves written all over your face, you were still beautiful."

Involuntarily, a tear had slipped from my eye because his memory of the day of my interview was impressive. I had the run in my stocking because Lamar and I had fought that morning, but I was determined to make it to the interview. I remember curling my hair, but because of the fight, it sweated out, which caused me to lay it down in a bun. I made eye contact with Patience but couldn't stop my eyes from watering.

"I know that I want *you,* Autumn. All of you. All sex aside, I want you in my life. You have your head on straight, and your soul is so pure. This vibe between us is like a breath of fresh air for me. I feel like you will really be something different not only for me but for my daughter as well," he confirmed.

I blew out a sharp breath. Dating Lamar was exhausting. I didn't want to end up in another mess like the one I had with him, but leaning over and kissing Patience felt oh so right. He cupped my face with his strong hand as our tongues intertwined.

Bang Bang Bang

The loud noise that came from my front door ended our steamy rendezvous. There was a feeling in the pit of my stomach that I couldn't get rid of. Patience looked at me, and that's when I remembered that we were in my house and that I should have answered the front door. I hoped like hell that it wasn't Lamar on the other side.

"Who is it?"

I should have been checking the Ring App on my phone before coming to the door, but moving quickly, I wasn't thinking.

"Delivery."

"You're expecting something?" he asked.

I turned around to face Patience.

"No," I admitted.

I opened the door when the person on the other end knocked again. The voice from the other side didn't sound like Lamar, so I figured I would take my chances. The Spanish man on the other side held an Edible Arrangement.

"Autumn?" He questioned.

"Yes," I confirmed.

"Here you go. Have a good day."

He quickly looked over my shoulder before making his exit. I stood in my doorway, momentarily holding the Edible Arrangement. I had this eerie feeling in the pit of my stomach that I just couldn't shake. I locked the door and took the fruit arrangement straight to the kitchen. There was no name on the card, just a simple *Sorry,* and that alone told me where it was from.

"Toss some of those cantaloupes and strawberries in a bowl, and let's finish watching *The Blacklist*."

Patience had startled me. With this delivery, I felt like Lamar wasn't too far behind. I wanted to end the evening with Patience because I thought Lamar would pop up at my house. Reluctantly, I stood in my kitchen, unsure of which direction to take in this situation. Unbothered, Patience entered the kitchen and washed his hands at the sink before grabbing a bowl from my dishrack. The card that came with the fruit he had tossed in the nearby garbage and started putting some of the fruit into a bowl.

He never once asked who it was from, although he knows my story. I'm sure he knew it was from my ex. I stood by silently as I watched him prep the bowl for us. He had opened my fridge and got us both a water bottle.

"Come on, love."

I was infatuated with a man who could lead, and in my own house, he was stating orders. I wouldn't dare say bark because something about his demeanor was soft. I was used to Lamar's ways; it was his way or the highway in his world. Being in the presence of a man who spoke and handled me the way Patience did was refreshing.

We both ended up back on the sofa. After binging damn near all of season four, I had done more yawning than I wanted to. We had both shared two more cups of wine, which probably made me sleepy.

"It's getting late. Get some rest, beautiful."

He said before he had kissed me on the forehead when he stood.

"Let me get going because Parker has practice early in the morning," he added.

Unknowingly, I had poked my bottom lip out because I would miss spending time with him. Usually, Sundays were observed for laundry, cleaning my house, and meal prepping for the week, but I wouldn't have minded putting all those chores on the back burner to spend time with him.

"Okay," I stood from the couch and pouted a bit.

"Pick ya lip up, beautiful. I'll see you on Monday."

I followed him to my front door and watched him put on his sneakers. When he opened the front door, he saw a bouquet of flowers on my welcome mat. Lamar was laying it on thick, and honestly, I felt like picking the flowers up and roofing them. Patience picked up the white roses bouquet and then handed it to me.

"To new beginnings, right?" he asked.

His facial expression let me know that this delivery was from him. One thing about apartment complexes in the South is that as long as you tailed the person in front of you, you also had access to the community. I assumed whoever delivered this had done that to get in because my phone never rang from someone punching in my access code. My eyes misted like they had been doing in his presence.

I couldn't even recall when he was on his phone long enough to place the delivery. I nuzzled my nose into the bouquet and then gave it a whiff. New beginnings did sure smell so damn good.

"Goodnight, Mr. Jacobs."

I said with a smirk as he stood on the other side of my door.

"Goodnight, Ms. McKinley."

He had left me with yet another forehead kiss. I watched him swagger to his car, and I knew he would have the craziest hold on my heart if I allowed him to. I closed my apartment door only when he made it safely to his car. Like a giddy schoolgirl, I ran over to my phone to call Amani.

When she didn't answer, I texted her to call me back, and then I started to clean off the coffee table that Patience and I had made a mess of. The way his scent still lingered in my living room had my womanly area throbbing.

After tossing the garbage away, I headed straight for my bed. My nightstand had many toys to get me where I needed to be. Before getting comfortable in bed, I grabbed my rose from the nightstand. With Patience on my mind, I entered a solo pleasing session that I knew would have me sleeping comfortably through the night.

Chapter 7

Amani Tate

I nervously tapped my finger on the table while waiting for Matthew's arrival. He said we needed to talk, so I sat at a table at one of our favorite breakfast spots. I hated waiting, and he knew that shit. Ten minutes was enough for me to grab my purse, head back to my car, and leave, but I needed to know what was so important that we had to meet and talk so early.

Lately, he had been distant, and I mean, between vacationing and his workload at work, I could see why, but something was off with him, and I just couldn't put my finger on it. The bell ringing on the door caused me to look up. Matthew quickly made his way over to me. Besides slacks and a dress shirt for work, he was a sweatsuit-wearing guy. I couldn't stop my eyes from roaming down and sneaking at his print before he took his seat.

"Sorry I'm late," he said, quickly picking up the menu and glancing at it.

Since we had frequented this spot quite a bit, I knew his mind was elsewhere. Something was troubling him, and I needed to know what was going on.

"What's up with you?" I asked.

"I have to stop seeing you."

His response caught me off guard. The spit in my mouth thickened, so I quickly reached for the glass of water the waitress had brought me while waiting for his arrival.

"Come again?" I asked for clarification once I got myself together.

"I have a fiancé and—"

"YOU HAVE A WHAT?"

I was yelling in the empty restaurant and didn't give a damn. I felt sick to my stomach. I had let a man into my body that belonged to someone else, and I didn't move like that. I didn't even play those games because I truly believed in karma.

I wasn't the sharing type, being the only child I never had to be. I looked deep into his dark brown eyes as we sat in silence. His eyes watered, and it took everything in me not to come across the table and hurt him. I didn't realize I had been crying until I felt the tear trickle down my cheek.

"Amani, I love you, I do. I just got caught up. I don't know what the fuck I'm doing anymore."

"Huahhhh," I openly breathed before speaking, "Bye, Matthew."

I stood and turned to walk away, but he grabbed my hand.

"Mani, please, I just need to figure this shit out."

I almost broke my own wrist, pulling it from his grasp.

"I'm good, love."

Once I was free of my hand, I walked out of the restaurant. I broke down when I reached the seclusion of my car's inside. Behind the tinted windows of my Acura, I ugly girl cried. I let a man unknowingly put me in a side bitch position, and I hated myself for it. I carried myself with respect. I wondered what was written across my forehead to make this man think that he couldn't treat me as such.

Frantically going through my bag, I searched for my cell phone. Matthew had called me three times. I blocked his number and then called Autumn from my missed calls log. She had called me the night before, but I was busy getting my hair and everything together to sit down with Matthew this morning.

"Hello?" Her voice sounded groggy.

I wasn't even sure if she was lying next to Patience, but I needed my best friend.

"He's engaged," I choked out.

"Come over," she urgently responded.

I ended the line and went to her house without saying anything else. The drive over my thoughts consumed me with how I had let something like that go undetected for almost a year. It's either his fiancé knew of his cheating ways, or I had been recoloring the red flags that were presented in front of me. On the way over to Autumn's, I mentally beat myself up. The audacity of the weather to shift to match my mood so perfectly.

The dark gray clouds started to slowly glide across the skies. Big raindrops hit my windshield rapidly after punching in the code to the gate and parking. I ran to Autumn's door, and it opened quickly. She had her arms out for a hug that I desperately needed.

"It's okay," she said soothingly, rubbing my back.

I let my tears out. I had to. Autumn had this big sister aura about her, and I knew I sometimes made terrible life decisions. Instead of hitting me with the, *I told you so* or chastising me, she was always the listening ear.

After our embrace, I left my shoes at the door and followed her to the living room. On the coffee table, I saw two bouquets of roses.

"He went all out. You must have given him some kitty," at the moment, I had to crack a joke to keep myself from becoming a crying mess again.

"Girl, shut up. Patience is just…" she let her words trail off and blushed slightly, "We aren't talking about him. Let's talk about Matthew. Do I need to slap the shit out of him tomorrow? Or do you wanna go in there and knock all that shit on his desk over? I'm with whatever."

Autumn was a ride-or-die for sure. In a room alone with any man of mine, I wouldn't have any worries except if she was going to body slam the nigga for the last time he made me cry.

"Na, you need the job, remember I don't. I'm just going to go ahead and quit."

"Mmm"

"We're still going to be besties," I said reassuringly.

"Mmm," she said again.

"Just say it."

Autumn had this thing about making sound effects when she couldn't quite find the words for something.

"So you're going to let this man run you away from a bag."

I came from money, and she knew this. My mother was a judge, and my father was a neurology surgeon. The only reason I had even gotten this job, to begin with, was because my parents were getting on my ass about how the age of thirty would be here before I knew it. I had nothing to show for it. They had me when they were both older, and with no older siblings as test dummies, I literally did what I wanted to do.

Although they both were driven and had the professions to prove it, neither one forced their goals or work ethic onto me. To be honest, what I was passionate about was doing hair, and I was damn good at it. With a hair page of over ten thousand followers, I was ready to turn one of my many side hustles into my primary source of income.

"Making my own money is nice, but what I'm doing right now is not what I'm passionate about."

She shook her head understandably and then offered me a smile. Autumn already knew that my real passion was doing hair.

"Okay, now I'm going to have to start making myself appointments when you blow up because you are talented."

I looked at the top of her head and saw her wearing a bonnet.

"You can always squeeze in with me," I said with a smile before scrunching my face up, "ummm, what's under there?" I asked.

"My hair is in a wrap. I need to go and get a silk press for real," she admitted.

"Let's slap one of your wigs on. You gotta look extra good for your man tomorrow."

Doing hair was therapeutic, and I knew I needed the distraction.

"Fine," she finally caved, "and he's not my man," she added.

"Not yet," I lightly sang as I got up from the couch and went to her bathroom.

Being there numerous times, I knew where she kept all her hair products. She had this bucket under her sink full of wigs. I fished through the bucket to decide which one to play with. I smiled brightly when my hands came across a 30-inch middle part bust down.

"Now, this I can work with," I said lowly.

After gathering everything I needed, I walked back into the living room and saw that she had one of her dining room chairs in the middle of the floor for me. She turned on some music, and then I got to work. With music blaring and conversation going on, Autumn provided an atmosphere I desperately needed. As I did her hair, she told me how she planned to give Patience a chance. My friend deserved her happily ever after, and I thought he would be the perfect fit for her.

We freely drank the last bit of wine she and Patience had left behind from the day before as I installed her hair. With our conversation, I could free myself of my confusion on the way over. One thing that was clear and evident was that I was done with Matthew's ass. I made it up in my mind that my main focus would be getting my hair business off the ground.

I had her hair nice and laid in no time, and I was on my way out the door. I had to go home to type up an email letting Matthew know that I was resigning and had to create a vision board for my company.

☙ ☙ ☙ ☙ ☙ ☙

Lamar

I scrunched my face up in annoyance when I saw Amani's hoe ass walking to her car. Since Autumn had started that job, there was a change in her, and everything in me wanted to blame Amani for it. She was young, slick at the mouth, and fucking annoying to me. I watched her pull off and sat in my car for a while, just evaluating how my life had turned out.

It was late in the afternoon, and I had taken the weekend off work since it was the anniversary of my mother's death. I never took it as hard as Luther, but it still stung a bit. He was her favorite, and I was the family's black sheep.

To know that she had committed suicide without me making her proud first pissed me off a bit. You never know the mental struggles that someone is going through because I never in a million years thought that she would have taken her own life. I felt that she loved herself too much for that, or at least I thought that she cherished her kids enough to overcome the battles that came with depression.

One thing that she did love while she was here was Autumn's ass. She used to tell me that she was the woman that I was supposed to marry. She used to say that Autumn was the one woman who would finally bring substance into my life. I took a few more moments to self-evaluate before leaving my car. I had tossed on some sweatpants, a t-shirt, and sneakers just to come over. I thought that Autumn would have at least texted a nigga yesterday, considering what the day was. Even after I had sent the edible arrangement the day before, I thought she would have reached out, but there was nothing.

When I reached her door and knocked, it immediately swung open. *I knew she missed a nigga,* I thought confidently as the door pulled open.

"Don't tell me you forgot your purse?" She said before even paying attention to who was on the other side of the door.

When we made eye contact, I could tell she regretted pulling the door open like that.

"Please leave."

"Can we talk?" I asked, totally ignoring her request.

She wore her headscarf tied tightly around her head, and her hair was pressed straight and ended right at her hips.

"There's nothing to talk about. Can you go?"

I looked over her shoulder and could see straight into the living room. The two bouquets of flowers in the vases that I had gotten her infuriated me. In a quick, swift move, I pushed her into the house and slammed the door behind me.

"Lamar, please get out of my house."

"You got a nigga here?"

Instantly, I thought about the dude I had pulled over the other night. Frantically, I started walking around the house, checking her bedroom, bathroom, and closets.

"No one is here. Just go!" She yelled, walking behind me.

I stopped dead in my tracks, and she followed so closely behind me that she ran into my back. When I saw the rose toy that she always kept inside the drawer of her nightstand on top of it, I lost it. She had only used that while I was deep in her guts.

Autumn wasn't the freaky type and never had been. She had gotten every little toy in that drawer because I had talked her into it. And here she was, showing the next nigga the tricks that I had taught her. Quickly, I turned around to face her.

"You gave my shit away, hmm?"

I grabbed her face, and I wanted to ball that shit up in the palm of my hand like a piece of paper. But instead, I just held a firm ass grip on her cheeks that kind of scrunched her face up.

"Get off me," she managed to say as she tried to fight me back.

I drug her ass all the way to her side of the bed and damn near tried to put her head through the nightstand. Honestly, I blacked out. My own grunting is what brought me back from my angry moment. I tended to do that a lot when I got angry to this point.

"I'm sorry," I whispered when I realized that I bashed Autumn's face on the nightstand numerous times.

The rose was now on the floor, and her blood was on the nightstand. She was lying on her back on the bed with her shirt torn open, and the long checkered pajama pants she was wearing were torn off her. My sweatpants were around my ankles, and my dick was out.

"Just go," she cried out.

We were both sweating, me from violating her and her from probably trying to fight me back. I wasn't sure if I had broken her nose or not, but both of her eyes were bruised.

"Baby, I'm sorry."

I hated it when my anger got the best of me. Just the thought of someone touching Autumn had driven me over the edge. In my mind, her body was for me and me only.

"Get out!" She screamed as she shied her battered body away from me.

I looked around, and the scene looked terrible. I could tell Autumn was putting up one hell of a fight because my forearms had scratches. I had violated her physically, and all abuse aside, I never forced myself on her. I honestly didn't know how we had gotten here.

"Leave," she cried out.

Swiftly, I had pulled my sweats back up to my waist and then hauled assed. I could hear Autumn's cries get further as I swiftly moved through the apartment toward the front door.

Chapter 8

Patience

I was so tied up with Parker yesterday that I didn't have the chance to speak to Autumn. I had texted her when I had gotten in the night before and got settled, but I figured she was asleep already. Getting to work early and before her was the goal this morning. The night before coming in, I stopped for a bouquet of white roses. I took one out and then took it to work with me. I left the remainder of the bouquet home for Parker since she did well at practice. I got her ready for school and then dropped her off before heading to work.

After unlocking the front door and turning on the lights, I dropped the Dunkin Donuts bag and the one white rose on Autumn's desk as I walked past to head toward my office. Over the past two years, I have noticed that for breakfast, her go-to food is sausage, egg, and cheese on a croissant from Dunkin.

I didn't have any cases for the day, so I would be going through the stack of quote requests on my desk. I looked at the watch on my wrist and saw that I had a good hour before everyone came trickling in. Some of me wanted to go to the gym, but some of me wasn't in the mood. I sat at my desk and then scrolled around on my phone.

I logged into Parker's content page and saw that one of her reels received a badge for reaching over ten thousand views. I quickly fished through the comments, liking every single one. I was trying to see if any teams had commented.

Look at my baby now that's pure talent...

One comment stuck out to me when I clicked the page, and I saw no one other than Parker's mother. Her page was public, so I could see she was now married and had a whole family. I don't know what she hoped to gain from her comment, but after deleting it, I blocked her page. I was fuming afterward because what kind of shit was that. I was thankful that I ran and operated Parker's Instagram page. Had I didn't, things could have gone left.

Thankfully, because of the love that my mother and I showered Parker with, she didn't ask many questions about her biological mom. But I knew that if Ayesha kept up with these stunts, Parker would soon ask some questions. I had to get to the bottom of this shit because to wait a decade to want to be a parent was sickening to me.

I wondered if she still had the same number after all these years. I know I did. I wanted to speak to her directly. I wasn't sure what was going on in her life that she felt the need to reach out to Parker, but I wanted it to be known that it didn't matter because she was not needed. I checked the time on my wrist and saw that Autumn and Amani should be rolling in at any minute. When I heard the front door to the office open, I stood from the seat behind my desk and then stood in my doorway. I wanted to see her facial expression when she saw her desk.

One thing about me is that when I was interested in somebody, I didn't shy away from publicly expressing that shit. I hoped that Autumn didn't have a problem with a little public display of affection because I was all for that. When I saw Matthew walk through the door, looking disheveled, I raised my eyebrow.

"You look like shit," I admitted when I noticed that his shirt was wrinkled as hell.

"I feel like it too."

"What's wrong with you?" I asked.

Instead of offering me a response, he just walked toward me, walked past me into my office, and sat down in one of the seats on the other side of my desk. It was time for me to play therapist. I sighed slightly before following behind him and closing my office door.

"I told Amani that I was engaged, and she stopped fucking with a nigga. And I mean hard, too. I done hit the blocklist and all," he blurted out before I could even sit down.

"You got court today?"

"Na," he responded.

I opened the top drawer of my desk and pulled out a small bottle of Camarena Reposado. After sitting it on the desk, I pulled two glasses from the same drawer and poured two double tequila shots. I slid one his way, and he caught it. We both took a sip from our cups before I offered him a response.

"Did you think she would continue to let you pursue her?"

"I mean… these niggas be having side bitches all the time. Why that can't work in my favor, huh?"

"Those same niggas be upfront from the get-go."

He twisted his face in annoyance. I knew my friend well, so I let him have a mini-tantrum before adding to my statement.

"Realistically speaking had she gone for that shit, you would have respected her less. I know you."

"You right," he admitted, "she not even here today. She really doesn't fuck with me. I hope I didn't mess up shit for you. I saw Autumn's desk on the way in here."

I turned my phone over, looked at the time, and realized that she was thirty minutes late. Autumn didn't strike me as a woman who would stop her money for someone else. I picked up my phone and called her, but it rang out. The next person on my list to call was Amani. She had written Matthew off, but hopefully, she would answer for me.

"Hello," she answered on the third ring.

I placed the phone on speaker before responding.

"Ms. Tate, are you not coming to work today?"

Mathew fixed his mouth to say something, but I felt one finger up to silence him.

"Good morning, Mr. Jacobs. I was getting this email together to send to you and Mr. Jackson. I do apologize for the short notice, but effective immediately, I would like to resign from the company for personal reasons."

I knew Amani had her ratchet ways, but she handled this like a big boss. For this girl to be young, she sure was professional.

"I understand. Well, don't worry about that email. I will relay the message to Matthew. Um, Amani, have you heard from Autumn?"

"Not since yesterday. Is she not there?"

"She isn't," I confirmed.

"Well, that isn't right. I just did her hair yesterday for work today. I'll call her once we get off the phone."

She had that same worry in her voice. The same concern she did when Autumn was late that one morning.

"Shoot me a text to let me know if you hear from her," I said.

"Got ya."

She ended the line, and when she did, Matthew slid his cup in my direction. I poured more into the glass before putting the rest of the bottle back into my drawer.

I got this funny feeling in my stomach, and I couldn't shake that shit.

"What's on your mind?" Matthew asked.

I knew I must have been wearing all my thoughts on my profile.

"Nothing," I shook off the funny feeling I had in my stomach.

"Do you have court today? He asked me the same question I had asked him a little while ago.

"Na."

"Go and check on your girl. I know how to answer phones."

He must have known that Autumn was on my mind.

"Umm, aight, I'll be back."

"See you tomorrow," he said as I grabbed my car keys and phone off my desk before rushing out.

When I got to Autumn's complex, I called the code she had given me days prior, but no one answered. When I noticed a car gaining access in front of me, I pulled closely behind it to make it through before the gate closed. I pulled up in front of her building and saw her Jeep parked outside.

Only then did I think about her having male company. Yes, I have expressed my heavy interest in pursuing her, but she doesn't belong to me since I haven't placed a title on things yet. Would I be wrong to ring her bell and she possibly have company over. I exited my car and headed to her front door because she didn't strike me as the type to juggle multiple men. I was about to ring the doorbell when I saw that her front door was slightly open. I took a deep breath before letting myself in.

Everything in me wanted to go back to my car to get the gun that I had purchased years ago as soon as I got a Georgia state license, but I didn't. One thing about me was that my hands worked, and they always have. I got a gun to begin with to protect me and Parker from any threat, but using one was never a go-to for me. I'll beat a nigga to a bloody pulp first and use a weapon as a last resort.

When you first walk into her apartment, you can see straight into the living room. Hair products were all over the coffee table, proving that Amani had been there the day before to do her hair. I walked toward her bedroom, and her door was slightly open. The quietness in the house gave me this eerie feeling. I was about to call her name out, but when I pushed the door and saw her back facing me, I didn't want to wake her without her seeing my face first.

"Hey beautiful, wake u—"

My words caught in my throat when I finally reached her side of the bed. Her blood covered the nightstand, and her pajamas were ripped. In front of me, she lay in a fetal position with her face and body battered and bruised.

"Autumn," I said lowly, crouching down to be at the same level as her.

Quickly, she jumped and spoke before even opening her eyes.

"Please, please just go."

She sounded like a baby as she was pleading with me, and instantly, I became angry because I wanted to hurt whoever had done this to her.

"It's Patience. Love, who did this to you."

She could barely open her swollen eyes, but I could see her trying.

"What are you doing here?"

I could see the tears sliding down her pudgy cheeks as she asked.

"Who did this to you, love?"

Although her body was exposed to me, I ignored all of that shit because I wanted answers. My heart was beating out my chest.

"I can't say."

"Can't or won't?" I asked with a raised eyebrow.

Whoever was responsible for this was the Walking Dead to me. The whimpers that escaped her body as she cried made me damn near break down with her. I decided then that me finding out who was responsible for this shit was going to have to wait.

"Shh, shh, okay. Okay," gently, I moved some of her hair out of her face. "Let's get you washed up, okay?"

She nodded her head up and down, and even that looked like it hurt.

"I'll be right back, okay?"

"Okay," she said it so lowly it was almost childlike.

After walking into her bathroom, I had closed the door behind me to give me the privacy that I needed to get my shit out. The strongest souls were often sent to the darkest places. I had seen my mother similar to this, and it was pulling the little boy's emotions out of me.

In front of her mirror, I let a couple of tears slip because women like her, women like my mother, didn't deserve shit like this. Women, period, never deserved some shit like this to happen to them. I used the back of my hand to wipe my face clean, and then I pulled back her shower curtain and ran some bath water on her.

After adding some of the bubble wash she had sitting on the side of the tub, I checked the water to ensure it was at a suitable temperature. She had a rag, towel, and robe on a rack behind the door, so I took the rag and towel down and placed it on the sink.

When I opened the bathroom door, she was still lying exactly how I had left her.

"Come on, love, let me help you up."

I helped her sit up in the bed. Her shirt was so badly torn that her breast was exposed. I didn't want to ask her to walk anywhere because I feared that would hurt her more.

I scooped her into my arms and carried her into the bathroom. On the way there, she gently laid her head on my chest. After helping her undress, I assisted her in easing down into the bath water. I saw that she had a bonnet hanging on the back door handle.

"Here, put on your little chef hat so you don't wet up more of your hair," she took the bonnet from me and let out a small chuckle. To allow the corners of her mouth to even turn up a little after what she had just been through was warrior shit in my eyes. I handed her the rag from the sink and then started to make my exit.

"Are you leaving?" She asked.

"No, love, I just need to make a couple of calls, okay?"

She nodded as she slowly started to dip her rag into her bath water. I closed the bathroom door behind me on the walkout to give her the privacy I was sure she needed. I quickly called my mother to explain what was happening and see if she could get Parker from practice for me. Without me having to go into too much detail, she agreed.

The next call I made was to Matthew. I needed a few days, and since I wasn't due to meet with a new client until the end of the week, I knew he wouldn't mind. While Autumn washed, I familiarized myself with her kitchen and found cleaning products under the sink. I cleaned off her nightstand and tried my hardest to get her blood out of the carpet beside her bed.

Seeing that her bed set was dirty, I stripped it. I tapped lightly on the bathroom door.

"Yes?" She responded.

I spoke through the door because she didn't give me access to open the door.

"Where are your sheets?"

"In the hallway closet."

Without a response, I headed that way and pulled a fresh set of sheets and a blanket out of the closet. After making her bed, I put the soiled sheets into her washing machine.

When I heard the shower water running, I figured that she was done soaking and ready to wash. I had gotten a text from Amani when I pulled up, letting me know that Autum did not answer the phone. A piece of me wanted to call her to find out who had done this. I was sure that if anybody knew she did, I wanted to give Autumn all my attention. She deserved that.

⚐ ⚐ ⚐ ⚐ ⚐ ⚐

Autumn

I feel like a Mack Truck had hit my ass. As I stood under the shower head, I let the beads hit me at the speed of two. I loved the custom showerhead I had made Lamar install when we moved here. Gently, I washed my face. I don't know why I was receiving a person like Patience at this point in my life, but I needed him.

I always knew that there was no good in Lamar, and after last night, I knew that his soul was evil. While I showered, I thought about going to the police station and reporting him. Putting his hands on me was one thing, but violating my body gave me a different kind of push that made me want him to pay for everything he had put me through.

Just thinking of him touching me without permission had me scrubbing my body so hard to the point where my skin felt raw. I knew that a person like him would never make it to heaven. A human being capable of what he had done would never make it to the upper room. He was going to the basement for sure. When my skin became too raw to touch, I rinsed it off for a final time and then turned the shower water off. I took my time getting out of the shower because I didn't want to lose my balance and hurt myself more.

After grabbing the towel on the sink, I dried my body off before wrapping it around my torso and tucking it under my arms. The steam in the room had fogged up the mirror, so I used my hand to wipe it to finally see the damage to my face. I know that I felt like shit, but I wasn't sure how badly I had looked.

A light gasp escaped my lips when I saw that both eyes were swollen and bruised. I had a broken nose before, and it didn't appear to be broken, but I had all intention of finding out when I had gone to the hospital. Thinking of how many times Lamar had bashed my face into the nightstand made me open my mouth quickly to make sure that I still had all of my teeth.

I felt a little relief that I hadn't lost any of the thirty-two. I grabbed my toothbrush, brushed my teeth, and rewashed my face. Taking off my towel and slipping into my robe, I kept glancing at my face. I couldn't believe that this was what Patience was subject to look at. I took a deep breath before leaving the bathroom.

"Hey, beautiful," he said once I entered my bedroom.

I could smell the cleaning products in the air. I felt like the furthest thing from beautiful, but I was in Patience's eyes. I had clean sheets on the bed, and that side of the room was restored.

"Thank you," was all that I could get out.

This man didn't have to do any of this, but he was. Men like him always deserved their flowers, so I had to give them to him. Patience Jacobs was the shit. I yawned, and I didn't even mean to.

"Sleepy, love?" He asked as he patted the side beside him on the bed.

Sleep couldn't fix this kind of tiredness. I was mentally and physically beaten. Lamar had done his biggest one; it was time for my lick back.

"I can't sleep, so I need to get dressed."

"Where are we going?" He asked as he stood from the bed.

By his actions, I could tell he wouldn't let me out of sight, at least for today.

"I need to go to the hospital and get a rape kit done, and then I need to go to the police station to file a report."

He had this blankness that came to his facial expression. It was evident that someone had beat my ass. I knew when he found me that I looked like a rag doll, but only I, Lamar, God, and now Patience knew what he had really done to me. His eyes had watered, and then I saw him blinking them away. His spadelike nostril flared. I could tell that he was trying to gain and keep his composure.

"Well, get dressed," he said, standing from my bed and walking toward the door. "I'll take you," he said before closing the door behind my room to give me the privacy I needed.

I walked to my closet and tossed out a pair of leggings, an oversized shirt, and some crocs. I wanted to be comfortable, especially since my body was still hurting.

"You ready to go, beautiful?" Patience asked when I had entered the living room. I grabbed my cell phone from the arm of the chair and was still surprised that it was powered on. I thought that the battery would have died by now. I saw all the missed calls from Patience and Amani, and I knew this private number was Lamar.

"Do you have a car charger?"

"Of course," he answered calmly as he held my door open for me.

I locked up, and then we made our way to his car.

The drive over to Emory Hospital was a silent one. I'm pretty sure that he was in his head like I was in mine. There wasn't even music that filled the car on the ride. He gently tapped his hand on the gear shift in the middle console. I put my hand on top of his. I was genuinely appreciative of everything that he was doing for me. He turned his hand over and then opened his palm. I placed my small hand into his, and he wrapped his hand around mine.

"Thank you," I said as he entered the hospital's parking lot.

"No need. I protect what I see as mine."

I couldn't offer a response. I was truly grateful because this man sitting beside me had done more for me than someone I had dealt with for years. He was an actual show that an amount of time didn't mean anything. A man who wanted to would, and since I had slightly stepped over the line of work and romance, he had pulled me onto that side with his strong arms, and he had shown every intention of keeping me there.

"You ready?" he asked when he cut the engine.

I let a sigh escape my mouth before I shook my head up and down. Hand in hand, we had walked into the hospital. We sat for about two hours before I was even seen. Having to repeat what had happened to me in front of him had my stomach knotting up, but I had to get it out. I intended to ruin Lamar's life, just as he had ruined mine.

"What happens next?" I asked Patience once the doctor and nurse were done examining me.

"Well, the nurse said she would return with your discharge papers. Next, you go to the police station and make an official report. They will most likely hit him with criminal charges. You have access to your ring camera, right?"

"I do," I confirmed.

"You're going to need that so they can have that evidence with your testimony."

"I'm kind of iffy on going to that specific police station," I admitted.

"Why?" His thick eyebrow raised, "I'm going with you. Does police presence bother you?"

"He's a cop."

He pulled his bottom lip in and squinted his eyes like he was thinking.

"What?" I asked when I could see his mind running rapidly.

"Nothing."

The nurse coming into the room to give me my discharge papers had cut off what I would ask him. I closed the curtain and then quickly changed back into my clothes. This was the part that I was battling with whether to report him or not.

We had our fights, but never have I turned out this bad. Never had Lamar forced himself on me. I let the tears slip down my face, just thinking about what was done to me. I hadn't realized that we had made it to the police station until Patience lightly touched my arm.

"You're strong. You got this love," he encouraged me when he had no idea I needed it the most.

I blew out a sharp breath before popping open the car door.

"You aren't coming with me?" I asked when I realized he hadn't turned the car off yet.

"Na, I need to handle a few things," he said as he lifted his phone from one of the cup holders in between the seats.

"Okay."

I was slightly disappointed but quickly brushed that off because everything he was doing all day, he didn't have to. I dragged my feet across the pavement as I entered the police station.

Chapter 9

Patience

I sat waiting in the car for Autumn to make her report. The only reason why I didn't go inside with her is that I honestly needed a moment to myself. With everything that she had been through, I decided to proceed. I still wanted her.

"Fuck!"

I roared out as I banged on my middle console.

Somebody had taken something from Autumn, and I wanted them in the dirt because of it. When she told me that her ex was a cop, I wondered if he was the same cop that had pulled me over the other night. I questioned how long he had been stalking her every move since their breakup.

Physically, she would heal. I was thankful for her that her nose wasn't broken. The impact of the nightstand on her face had made both her and her eyes swell. What wasn't going to heal over time was her spirit. He had broken that piece of her, and I swear I wanted to put him down for it. Knowing that she was attacked in her own home had me ready to take her away from that unstable, toxic environment.

A person should always feel safe under their own roof. I grabbed my phone and then booked a nearby Airbnb for the month. Something told me that once this crazy ass nigga got a whiff of her doing a report that he would be back at her house. At least she wouldn't be there for it.

Still not knowing who the dude was, I wanted to call Amani to get the scoop on him because if anybody knew about him, I knew she would. My thumb hovered over her name, and I quickly changed my mind when I remembered Autumn had been through something traumatic. She trusted me enough to share what had happened to her with me.

With prying about her ex, I would have to tell her what she told me, and I would never break her trust in me by doing that. I bit the bottom of my lip in anger because I would have to let this shit go, for now, that is. My phone vibrating in my hand brought me back from my thoughts. My mother was calling me. I explained the situation earlier so she could pick up Parker for me.

"Hello," I answered.

"How is she?"

My mother had this worry in her tone that only a mother could have. She had this caring spirit, and whatever or whoever I cared for, she did as well.

"We left Emory not too long ago. We're at the police station now. She's inside doing a report," I updated her.

"Mmm, some men try and take beautiful girls away from this world."

Coming to my job numerous times, she had a couple of run-ins with Autumn and always spoke highly of her professionalism.

"Yeah… in her own house is just," I had paused because my voice was breaking. I couldn't get over that shit.

"Get yourself together to be strong for her. I got Pumpkin for the rest of the week if you want to spend time with her. Trying to deal with that and keeping up with these practices will spread you thin."

Shit like that is what made my mother the goat in my eyes. Women before Autumn would frown upon her ways in stepping up exactly how she was now.

"Thank you, ma."

"You're welcome. You be careful you hear me. If that man can do something like that to a woman he loves, he won't care about taking your life."

She did have a point. I opened my middle console to make sure that my gun was there. The situation that Autumn was in was so unpredictable that I was playing with fire by even being in her presence.

"I'll be home sometime today to get me some clothes."

"We'll be here."

She told me that she loved me before ending the line.

Now that I had a temporary living arrangement for Autumn squared away for the next month, I had to handle business with work. Since the week consisted of paperwork, I made a mental note to stop by the office and gather whatever documents I needed for the week.

"How did it go?" I asked Autumn once the light in my car went off. I locked my phone and placed it back into the cup holder to give her my undivided attention. She sighed like the weight of the world rested on her shoulders, and in the moment, I knew that was exactly how it must have felt for her.

"It's done. I just don't know what happens now?"

I put the car in drive and then headed toward her house.

"Well, I'm sure they will start their investigation, but things aren't ending well for him. Now, we go to your place and pack you some stuff because I have somewhere for you to stay for the time being. Now you start over."

I looked her way and could tell she was at a loss for words.

"Is that okay with you?" I asked as I switched to the next lane.

I had known the way back to her house because my memory was so good.

"Yeah," she wiped away a tear that slid down her eye, and then, for the remainder of the drive over to her house, we both were quiet in the car.

Autumn

Patience waited in the car while I went into the house and packed some things into suitcases. He wouldn't tell me where I would be staying, but judging by his taste, it wouldn't be a hole-in-the-wall spot. I packed away some work clothes because once my face healed, I had every intention of going back to work. I needed the money because, at the end of the day, I still had bills. I appreciated everything Patience was doing for me. Still, I needed to get back to the girl who could and was doing it alone.

Lamar had spoiled me in a sense as well because being with him had knocked me off my independent throne. I was really the It Girl in college, and I let him come along and strip me of that. After packing one suitcase, I rolled it out into the living room. I started to pack some toiletries into the next one.

"Is this one ready to go, love?"

I could hear Patience's voice yelling from the living room.

"Yeah, wait, babe, take this too."

I quickly stuffed purses and some accessories into a duffle bag of mine before walking it out to the living room.

"So, I got upgraded to babe?"

He wore the sexiest grin on his face after he asked.

"I guess you did, huh?" I said with a little smirk at the end.

Making the facial expression hurt. Patience probably could tell because his eyes had softened while looking at me. Before I knew it, he had crossed the room and stood directly before me. He took the duffle bag from me and then stared at me intently.

"He deserves to be handled."

"I know," I admitted.

For so many years, Lamar had shown me that he didn't care if I breathed, so his livelihood was the furthest thing from my mind.

Patience gently cupped the side of my face. He was careful not to apply too much pressure. I could tell that he was being this soft with me out of fear of hurting me. He treated me like a fragile little bird, and I was soaking up every minute. People treated me like I was supposed to carry every burden and heartbreak on my back, which was truly exhausting.

With him, I knew there would never be a moment when I would bear all the problems. He was the type to take half, if not all, of any burdens that would come my way.

"Let me handle him for you."

I knew that he was serious because he was staring me dead in the eyes. Something about Patience screamed hood nigga. I didn't know much about Orange, New Jersey, but he carried himself like the men from back home.

The difference between him and them is that I could tell that he had polished himself up for society. He was a reserved hood nigga, and the northerner in me couldn't help but notice. Unlike most men back home, he had so much to lose. He was a respected lawyer and had a daughter. I relaxed my head in the palm of his hand. It didn't matter that the touch alone was paining me.

His eyes were pleading with me. I knew that he would take someone's life for me for me, but I couldn't and wouldn't let him do it.

"We will let the law deal with him. The same law that he took an oath to uphold and honor will be the same one that will turn its back on him. Mark my words."

That badge had protected him for so long, but I knew all that would end.

Patience seemed to be a little disappointed with my response. Still, he just nodded before grabbing the suitcase and taking it out. I returned to my bedroom and started to pack some more clothes. I stood for a while, just looking at my side of the bed. I knew that the whole situation must have given me PTSD.

I didn't know how to get over that aspect, but I knew that things would become more manageable with time. I didn't know exactly how the process of this investigation with Lamar would work. Still, I knew that whatever he had coming to him, he deserved it.

Chapter 10

Lamar

Six months later…

"Give you my badge and weapon. What?"

I must have been hearing my Captain wrong. For the past six months, I have been under investigation by the department. I knew that what I had done to Autumn was terrible, and over the past months, I had been seeing a therapist because of it.

"Officer Hoover, calmly and gently place your badge and weapon on the corner of my desk. Our superiors are at the end of their investigation. Still, the decision has been made to suspend you without pay until further notice. Hopefully, you will get your badge back when they are done."

I took my gun off my waist and placed it and the badge onto the corner of the desk in front of me. My Captain leaned in his chair to grab the items and put them inside his desk.

"I told you that I couldn't sweep your personal life under the damn rug anymore," he sucked his teeth out in frustration, "you have put me in the tightest of spots. I now have investigators poking their noses in places where they don't belong. They are finding holes in my department that would never have been noticed had you not gone off the deep end."

I was disappointed in myself just as he was, if not more.

"What do I do now?"

I genuinely wanted an answer to my question. Autumn had left me. Because of the charges brought against me, my brother wasn't fucking with me anymore, and now I didn't even have a fucking job.

"Live your life the best you can before the prosecution decides to execute."

His tone was disgusted, and I honestly didn't blame him. His eyes were focused on the picture frame on his desk. He was staring at the picture of his two grown daughters. What I had done was unforgivable. Over the past six months, I had been in and out of the courtroom, and every time, Autumn showed up with her lawyer nigga in tow.

He must have gotten her in touch with the best of the best because the prosecution lawyer had her foot on my neck, and she was not letting up. I knew that I needed help, and that's when talking to a therapist had entered my mind. My therapist and I had been going over why I had put myself in these situations. I still didn't have an answer to that one.

Before my dad had left, I had grown up in a home where he knew how to make his woman submit, and that was by any means necessary. In therapy, I learned witnessing that had created a norm in my head of how a relationship should go. I was thankful for my captain because he had protected me this far when he didn't have to. It was on me that he could no longer sweep my bullshit under the rug.

"Thank you," I said before turning around and preparing myself to exit.

I had to get myself ready to do the walk of shame. All the other officers had started the whispers when I walked past as soon as this investigation had come to light. I knew they would be huddled with one another, talking under their breath, when I exited.

"Hoover?"

"Yes, sir?"

I turned around to give my captain my undivided attention.

"You don't have any other weapons in your possession, right? Being suspended, you can not have any firearms."

"No sir," I looked that man straight in his eyes and had lied.

In the side panel of my truck outside, I had a .45 tucked away. These little niggas in Atlanta loved robbing people, and I'll be damned if I ever got caught slipping.

"Alright, well, I'm sure that your lawyer will keep in touch," he turned his attention back to the phone in his hand. My lawyer wasn't worth a damn, but at least I had one.

I continued walking out of his office. As I expected, everyone had started their whispers with my exit. Who I thought were my friends had turned their back on me. The charges against me weren't light ones either. First-degree rape and aggravated stalking were the two heinous crimes that I was faced with. A host of minor charges were tacked on as well. Autumn had her foot on a nigga's neck, and she wasn't letting up.

With everything going on in my life, I didn't even realize today was her birthday. Because the state had put a stay-away order in place, I couldn't drop anything at her front door to one, apologize, and, two, wish her a happy birthday. Since we had moved from up north, her favorite place to go was Hobby Lobby.

Since I couldn't be around her, I hopped in my truck and went there. It was the closest I was going to get to her. I couldn't even give her a call because that would land my ass in some kind of trouble. Walking around the store's aisles would bring back so many memories of me occupying my phone while she glided through the aisles, adding stuff to our cart.

A light smile came across my face as I parked and exited my truck. I grabbed a cart on the way in because I needed to decorate the tiny one-bedroom apartment I was forced to get once Luther had cut ties with me. Autumn had taught me the beauty in art and how it could turn a house into a home.

Everywhere we moved, she put her own little taste into every room of the house. I was in the aisle of the picture frames when I looked to my right and saw her. She was crouched down, looking through the styles on the second shelf. Before opening my mouth, I had just admired her beauty. Her natural hair was in loose curls. It was her birthday, and instead of all of the glitz and glam that other bitches were into, she settled for the more simple things.

The spit caught in my mouth as I tried to find the words. Autumn was so oblivious to me at the end of the aisle, staring at her. Her phone started ringing, and she quickly reached into her jeans' back pocket to answer.

"Yes, babe, I am coming right now. They don't have the frame that I want for our portraits."

After her statement, I realized that bringing that nigga to court wasn't to get back at me. She had genuinely moved on. I could feel my blood boiling. My life was in fucking shambles, and to me, it looked like she had been living her best life. I had no family, no job, I barely had a fucking roof over my head, and there she was glowing and happy in front of me.

I had counted in my head and controlled my breathing, a technique I learned in therapy. It was no secret that I had an anger problem. It was what landed me in the predicament that I was currently in.

"Yes, I am coming," she said before ending the line.

"Autumn," I wanted to get the chance to apologize.

She quickly stood from her crouching position and then looked in my direction. I could see the fear quickly build in her eyes, and I felt like shit because of it. I honestly just wanted to apologize.

"I just wanna say—"

"Help!" she yelled loud as hell, cutting me off.

The last thing I wanted was for attention to be drawn to us.

"Autumn, please."

"Somebody help me!"

She left her full cart in the middle of the aisle and then ran off. I took off running behind her. I just wanted to shut her up. She was moving so fast that she had to slow up in front of the automatic doors because she was moving faster than the doors could open.

Still, I was on her heels and wanted to catch her before she could get to her car. I just wanted her to know that I was sorry. She ran toward my truck, but I didn't see her jeep.

"Help!"

I really wished that she would quit all that yelling shit. When I saw the same ass lawyer nigga rushing out of the driver's seat of the midnight blue Benz that I had pulled him over in a couple of months back, I had lost it.

What were the odds that my truck was parked two cars down from his car?

"Are you okay?" I could hear him ask her.

The worry in his voice made me fume. Quickly, I yanked open the driver-side door of my truck and then grabbed my gun from the side of the door. I literally had nothing to lose. What was special to Autumn had to go. All of that sorry shit had left my body, and as I looked at them with anger in my eyes, I knew that it wouldn't return.

☨ ☨ ☨ ☨ ☨

Patience

Watching Autumn run full speed towards the car had my heart gallop in my chest like racing horses. I could see her mouth moving, but I couldn't hear the words coming out because the music in the car was so loud. I rushed out of the car, leaving the door open behind me.

"Are you okay?" I quickly asked as she ran into my embrace.

I don't know what had occurred inside of that damn Hobby Lobby, but I was ready to go back in there and handle whatever for her. I'll slap the shit out of an employee and then drag them into the parking lot by their collar for her.

Over the past six months, we have built a relationship. Parker and my mother had loved her. It was her special day, her birthday, and instead of dressing up and going out, she wanted to go decoration shopping for our new place. The simple things about her made me fall in love during the last six months.

"He followed me out here," she whispered.

I had to damn near strain my ears to hear her.

"Who?" I quickly asked.

"So, was this nigga around the entire time?"

I looked over Autumn's head and saw that it was her ex, Lamar. I never got the confirmation I wanted when everything occurred because she had to heal. The last thing that I wanted to do was add to her trauma or reopen wounds that she had closed.

My accusations of him being the same officer who had pulled me over were confirmed when I started going to court with her.

In a swift movement, I had moved her behind me when I saw that he had a gun in his hand. He must have lost his shit because it was broad daylight, and he had a gun pointed our way. It was evident that he had nothing to lose. I looked across the parking lot and saw people running to their cars. He was causing a scene, so I figured the police would be there for us in no time.

"Was this nigga around the entire time?"

He asked again as he pointed the gun at the same time.

"No," I heard Autumn answer behind me.

"Don't answer a damn thing from him."

I stood firmly. Judging by the gun in his hand, I knew that even as an officer, he wasn't shit but a bitch in a badge. Without that gun in front of him, I knew that I would beat the shit out of him. How he gripped the handle tightly, let me know he probably felt the same way.

He was on crash-out status, so I knew that in his mind, this situation was more than likely an end all be all.

"You telling her what to do when I'm the one with the gun in my hand is a stupid move, bruh."

I sighed in relief when I heard the sirens in the distance. Autumn stepped from behind me.

"Just go!" she yelled.

"And leave you with this nigga? Na..."

How his facial expression turned stiff, and his eyes went cold let me know what he was on. I didn't have time to react and reach into the car for my gun because the shot went off so fast, followed by the second.

Boom... Boom

Seeing Autumn jump more in front of me, moved in slow motion. She fell into my arms after the two shots.

"No!" he yelled out.

The sirens seemed to be closer. In shock, I stood with Autumn in my arms. I could tell that she was bleeding heavily because the jacket that I wore started to soak in her blood.

"Autumn?" I said just above a whisper.

When I looked up at who had shot her, he still held the smoking gun in his hand.

Chaos had erupted in the parking lot all because of him. I closed my eyes and welcomed the bullet that he would send my way.

Boom...

I had never been shot before, so I'm sure the no pain must have been me in shock. When I opened my eyes, I could see him sprawled out on the floor. *This nigga shot himself,* I thought to myself.

And it's forever, so I hope you never up and bail
And if you ever left me for someone, you gon' get
someone killed

The radio from my car was playing in the background. Bystanders in the parking lot looked on. I heard the sirens getting closer, but they weren't close enough for me.

"HELP!" I cried out.

There was so much blood coming from Autumn's body. Tears clouded my vision as I cradled her body in my arms before yelling out again.

"Somebody help me…"

To be continued…

Forever My Man

COMING SOON

Made in the USA
Coppell, TX
27 November 2024

41136852R00111